J. T. EDSON'S
FLOATING OUTFIT

The toughest bunch of Rebels that ever lost a war, they fought for the South, and then for Texas, as the legendary Floating Outfit of "Ole Devil" Hardin's O.D. Connected ranch.

MARK COUNTER was the best-dressed man in the West: always dressed fit-to-kill. BELLE BOYD was as deadly as she was beautiful, with a "Manhattan" model Colt tucked under her long skirts. THE YSABEL KID was Comanche fast and Texas tough. And the most famous of them all was DUSTY FOG, the ex-cavalryman known as the Rio Hondo Gun Wizard.

J. T. Edson has captured all the excitement and adventure of the raw frontier in this magnificent Western series. Turn the page for a complete list of Berkley Floating Outfit titles.

J.T. Edson

THE REBEL SPY

BERKLEY BOOKS, NEW YORK

THE REBEL SPY

A Berkley Book/published by arrangement with
Transworld Publishers Ltd.

PRINTING HISTORY
Corgi edition published 1968
Berkley edition/March 1987

ISBN: 0-425-09646-7

A BERKLEY BOOK® TM 757,375
Berkley Books are published by The Berkley Publishing Group,
200 Madison Avenue, New York, NY 10016.
The name "BERKLEY" and the stylized "B"
with design are trademarks belonging to
Berkley Publishing Corporation.

PRINTED IN THE UNITED STATES OF AMERICA

For Roy Toon, The Demon P.H.G.

CHAPTER ONE

A Uniform of Cadet-Grey

While Captain Wormold, 5th Illinois Cavalry, did not profess to be a nervous man, he decided that he would feel a whole heap happier on completion of his present assignment. Not only did he have to take three wagons and a Rocker ambulance loaded with supplies across Arkansas to the Indian Nation outposts, but the real high brass saddled him with that damned runty civilian and gave all kinds of orders regarding his safety.

Any Union Army officer looked on supply-escort duty with misgivings. The rebels might be meeting with defeats back East and the tide of the War apparently turning in favour of the Union, but in Arkansas the Southerners gave no sign of following the general trend. From the time General Ole Devil Hardin assumed command over the Confederate States' Army of Arkansas, he not only halted the Yankee advance across the Bear State but inflicted defeats and held the Union Army on the verge of retreat. Given more men, arms, equipment, Ole Devil might even have pushed the enemy back, but the South could supply no further aid. So he held his position on the western banks of the Ouachita River and forced the Yankees to expend efforts that could be better used in breaking down resistance in the main Southern States.

The Northern States used their industrial superiority to produce new weapons and means of waging war. Already their blockade of the South threatened the Confederate's existence. New Orleans and much of the lower Mississippi lay in Yankee hands. While European countries might be willing to trade supplies for Southern cotton, the U.S. Navy held down the shipments to a minimum.

Despite all his difficulties, Ole Devil Hardin held on in Arkansas. Just a shade bitterly, Wormold realised that the North helped make Ole Devil's success possible. Wanting to strike down the heart of the South, the Federal Government concentrated its main efforts on the eastern battle-fronts. Little could be spared to allow the Union soldiers in Arkansas to regain their ascendancy over the rebels. Supplies came, but a tendency developed to withdraw seasoned troops to go East and replace them with raw, inexperienced men. Matched against the battle-tried veterans of the Confederate Army, who fought in conditions really suited to their ways, the superior numbers of the North achieved nothing.

More than that, it seemed the rebels relied on the Union Army to supply them with the specialised needs of an army in the field. Being Texas-born, the majority of Ole Devil's command were past-masters in the Napoleonic art of making war support war. Trained almost from birth by war against Indians, they turned the redskins' tactics to their advantage and, using the methods of their enemies, drew their needs from the unwilling hands of the Yankees.

A supply convoy like the one under Wormold's protection carried many items which the rebels would only be too pleased to acquire. Which accounted for why a full troop rode as its escort. While Wormold's troop fell some thirty short of the desired one hundred men complement, they

carried Sharps carbines—the best general-issue arm at that
time available—and, he believed, could put up a respectable
defence against the normal run of rebel raiding force.

Of course other men had felt the same way; only to return
in shame with a tale of soldiers killed and badly-needed
supplies swept off to further the Southern cause.

Wormold felt again the bitterness at a fate which put him
on the Arkansas battlefront when most of his West Point
class-mates served in the East, with its attendant chances
of distinction and acclaim. There would be little credit given
at the successful conclusion of the escort duty, unless he
should also bring off a victorious defence against raiding
rebels. Even then the news would rate only a couple of
columns on the inside pages of the important Eastern newspapers; and not even that should more important news be
available.

Should he fail to bring off the assignment due to enemy
action, it would be remembered against him beyond all
proportion to recognition for success. So Wormold determined to take no chances. All day he kept his best men—
a relative term when so few veterans were available to stiffen
the ranks of green recruits—out on the flanks, ahead and
to the rear, and receive no reports of sighting the enemy.
By pushing the wagons hard, he hoped to have passed beyond the area in which the rebel cavalry concentrated their
main efforts.

When night came, he set up camp on the shores of a
small lake. While he might have hoped for more open land
around him, he realised that such would not be available
even should he push on after watering the horses. A career
soldier, Wormold knew his business and went about it in
the dying light of day. Holding half his command as a grand
guard by the wagons, he split the remainder into four picket
sections and sent each group out some five hundred yards
on the major points of the compass. Nor did they form the
sole defence. Each picket placed out an arc of three vedettes,
mounted sentries, between three and four hundred yards

beyond them. Finally two mounted men rode a beat between each picket and the grand guard. Wormold would have a tired command the following morning, but felt the means justified the end as another day's hard travel ought to see them in safe territory.

Setting up the pickets and establishing the vedettes took time, and called for the efforts of Wormold, the first and second lieutenants, first sergeant, five sergeants and three corporals. Standing by the fire built for him, Wormold glanced at his watch and found the time to be almost ten o'clock. Cooking pots bubbled on section fires and steam rose, wafting the tempting aroma of coffee, from the muckets, as the troopers called the small 3-pint capacity kettles issued to them. Although the carbines had been piled by the men, they stood close enough to hand should an alarm be raised by one of the circle of watching sentries.

Satisfied that he had taken every precaution to safeguard the convoy, Wormold decided to join his two subordinate officers as they sat chatting to the small, dapper civilian who perched, as always, on the wooden box which formed his most prominent item of luggage. Wondering what might be in the carefully locked and watched-over box, Wormold became aware of a man walking from the darkness towards him. While he realised that something was wrong, his mind refused to accept the obvious answer given by his eyes.

Man might not be the correct term for the newcomer, for he looked to be in his late 'teens. Although not more than five foot six in height, his shoulders had a width that hinted at strength and he tapered down to a slim waist. His uniform differed in a number of respects from that worn by the 5th Illinois Cavalry. Not his boots, or tight-legged riding breeches, at first glance, for they conformed to regulations, even to the cavalry-yellow stripe down the pants legs. First major difference was his weapon belt. It hung a shade lower than usually seen, two matched white-handled Colt 1860 Army revolvers butt forward in holsters that not only lacked a top but left half the cylinder and all the trigger-guard exposed while being built to the contours of the guns. That started the difference. The tunic carried them even further. Ending at his waist, it lacked the skirt "hanging half-way between hip and knee", had a double row of buttons and stand-up collar which bore on either side triple three-inch long, half-inch wide gold braid bars; these served instead of decorated epaulettes as a means of knowing the wearer's rank. Instead of a cravat, the newcomer had a tight-rolled scarlet silk scarf which trailed its ends down over his tunic. Shoved back on his head, a white Davis campaign hat showed curly, dusty blond hair and a tanned, handsome young face with lines of strength and determination etched on it. The hat carried a different insignia to the United States shield inside a half wreath and bearing a bugle with the letter 'M' in its handle ring, being, like the Texas coat of arms, a five-pointed star in a circle.

Despite a growing tendency to standardise uniforms and equipment within the Union Army, some regiments still retained their individual style of dress. A few continued to wear sleeve decorations, but not that double braid 'chicken-guts' adorning the small newcomer's arms. And no *Federal* outfit wore uniforms coloured cadet-grey.

Still Wormold could not credit his eyes with seeing correctly, even though everything he saw told him the other did not belong to any *Yankee* regiment.

"Howdy, Captain," greeted the small newcomer, his voice a pleasant Texas drawl. "That coffee sure smells good."

"Coff—!" began Wormold, all coherent thought struck from him by the sight of a captain in the Texas Light Cavalry calmly strolling into a Union camp.

From their lack of reaction to the sight, his men failed to realise their danger. Wormold let out a low hiss and reached towards his holstered revolver. The small Texan's left hand made a sight-defying flip across to and drew the right side Army Colt, thumbing back the hammer and sliding the forefinger on to the trigger as, not before, the barrel cleared leather and slanted towards Wormold. In a bare three-quarters of a second Wormold found himself looking into the levelled muzzle of a cocked revolver. The Yankee captain's hand had not even reached the flap of his holster.

"Your camp's surrounded, Captain," warned the Texan. "I don't want to kill your men, so tell them to surrender."

Already the occupants of the camp realised that something *far* out of the ordinary was taking place. Realisation did not bring reaction fast enough. By the time the Yankees shook themselves out of the shock caused by the small Texan's appearance, they learned he did not come alone. Suddenly, rising out of the ground it seemed, grey-clad soldiers appeared holding lined guns. Wormold needed only one swift glance to know the futility of resistance. Long before his men could reach their piled carbines, or draw revolvers, Texas lead would tear into them. Nor did the casually competent manner in which the Texans handled their weapons lead him to believe that they lacked ability in the shooting line. There might be a chance if—

"We'd've been here sooner," drawled the small Texan and killed Wormold's hope stone dead. "But it took us time to nail down all your pickets and vedettes." Then his voice took on a harder tone as his eyes, darting from point to point, saw something of importance. "Tell that green shave-tail to sit fast before he dies a hero and gets a lot of men killed for no good reason."

The warning came just in time. Already Wormold's second lieutenant, showing more courage than good sense or judgment of the situation, tensed and sent his hand creeping towards his holster. If the shavetail drew, he would die and in doing so provoke an incident that might easily see Wormold's entire troop wiped out.

No coward, Wormold was also not a fool. He must balance the lives of the majority of his men against the very slender chance of saving the convoy. There could be only one answer. Surrender, let the wagons be taken, but save his men to fight another day.

"Sit still, Mr. Benson!" he barked. "Get your hand away from that gun."

"Now that's a whole heap more comfy," the small Texan remarked as Benson obeyed. "I'd be obliged, Captain, if you'd order your men to lie face down on the ground and with hands spread out."

Sucking in a bitter breath, Wormold gave the required command and watched his men obey it. Maybe his troops lacked veterans, but the men recognised the danger well enough not to resist the small Texan's wishes.

"Pluck their stings, Cousin Red," the Texan told his tall, well-built, freckle-faced and pugnaciously handsome first lieutenant, a youngster no older than the rebel captain and with a thatch of fiery red hair showing under his campaign hat.

Clearly every detail had been arranged. Without waste of time, half-a-dozen men moved forward under the lieutenant's command to collect the piled carbines and remove revolvers from Yankee holsters.

"Sharps linen cartridge breech-loaders, Cousin Dusty," enthused the lieutenant. "These boys're loaded for bear."

While the linen-cartridge firing Sharps lacked the Henry or Spencer repeaters' rate of fire, ammunition for them could be made in the South. So the Sharps found greater favour than the more advanced guns, which needed metal-case bullets, items only obtainable through the enemy and in short supply even there.

"We'll requisition them then," smiled the small Texan. "See them guarded, Red. Billy Jack, check what's in the wagons."

"Yo!" answered the tall, gangling, miserable-looking rebel sergeant major. "It's about time the Yankees shipped out some decent guns for us."

"I reckon I'd best have the officers' guns while I'm at it," remarked the lieutenant.

"It'd likely be best," agreed the Texas captain.

While handing over his weapon belt, Wormold raked his captor from head to toe with disbelieving eyes. Having heard the small Texan's first name, a thought sprang immediately to mind; yet Wormold wondered if it could be possible.

Could that small, almost insignificant appearing young-ster—he would be no more than eighteen, and a young eighteen at that—be the man rated by many as among Dixie's top three fighting cavalry commanders? Was it pos-sible that he might be the rebel who, in Arkansas, stood even higher than Turner Ashby or John Singleton Mosby? The man who voluntarily went behind the Union lines to give evidence at the court-martial of a Yankee officer falsely accused of cowardice and while there killed a much-disliked Federal general in a duel.* Or he whose raids over the Ouachita left havoc in their wake, while causing many a Yankee officer of great age and seniority to curse in impotent rage and wish he fought a more orthodox enemy.

Looking at the smart, disciplined efficiency of the Tex-ans, Wormold concluded that he guessed right. By the worst kind of lousy luck, he had fallen foul of Dusty Fog. The smoothness with which the whole affair had been carried out showed a dash and flair few men could produce. Effi-ciency of that kind came only through excellent leadership. Not an imaginative man, Wormold could still almost picture the silent stalking which captured his vedettes and pickets before any of them might sound the alarm. That alone called for a degree of planning and organisation far beyond the normal run of officers.

"May I join you at supper after we've finished, Captain?" asked the small Texan. "My name is Fog, Captain Dustine Edward Marsden Fog, at your service—up to a point."

"I called it right!" Wormold screamed mentally. "He *is* Dusty Fog!" Then he stiffened into a brace. Hell's fire; he would be externally damned if he allowed that rebel kid to out-do him in courtesy, or allowed the others to see just

Told in "The Fastest Gun in Texas."

how he felt about being captured. So he drew himself to a brace and saluted. "It'll be my pleasure, Captain Fog, Wormold, Captain Rupert Ainsley Wormold."

Moving forward, Dusty's bugler gathered up Wormold's discarded weapon belt and looked into its holster. "It's a Starr, Cap'n Dusty," he said in a disgusted tone, showing the revolver.

"Unload it and put it back," Dusty answered and holstered his Colt.

One of Red Blaze's section stood alongside Lieutenant Benson, holding the officer's highly-prized Spencer carbine in his hands. Still seated, Benson glared fury up at the soldier as the latter spoke to Dusty.

"This here's a mighty fancy gun, Cap'n Dusty."

"Damn you!" Benson spat, face twisted in anger and mortification. "My mo—."

At a signal from Dusty, the soldier tossed the carbine over. As he claimed, it proved to be a fine piece, with a better finish and furnishings than the usual run of issue carbines.

"A private arm, mister?" Dusty asked.

"Yes—sir," Benson replied, the second word popping out before he could stop it.

"His mother presented it to him, Captain Fog," Wormold explained in a low voice.

Opening the magazine trap, Dusty caught the spring, slid it clear and tipped seven bullets from the tube into his palm. Pocketing the bullets, he worked the lever which formed the triggerguard and ejected the round from the breech. Then he offered the carbine butt first to Benson.

"With my compliments, mister," Dusty said and nodded to the special pouch containing ten loaded magazine tubes. "I'll have to take your ammunition, though."

"Thank you, sir," Benson answered and this time there was no hesitation in using the formal honorific.

"What's in the wagons, Billy Jack?" Dusty called, leaving Benson.

"Powder, lead, made bullets, linen cartridges for a starter, Cap'n Dusty," answered the sergeant major, sounding as mournful as if they were the prisoners and about to lose the convoy. "General stores in the others."

"Take them when we pull out," ordered Dusty. "Go through the Rocker ambulance and turn out the medical supplies. Take one third of them."

"A third?" Wormold could not stop himself from saying.

"We're short on medical supplies, too, Captain," Dusty replied. "But I figure you have more casualties needing tending than we do."

Which, unpalatable as the thought might be, was perfectly true. Wormold felt a growing admiration for the small, young Texan and began to appreciate how Dusty won fame at an age when he should have just been starting in a military academy. The feeling did little to numb Wormold's sense of failure, however. Dusty Fog could act with his usual chivalry; return a mother's gift; prevent looting of personal property and abuse of captives; take only such medical supplies as his people needed; but he would leave Wormold's command without weapons, horses or equipment when he pulled out.

Already the disarmed Yankees had been allowed to sit up in lines, watched over by alert sentries. At the horse lines a sergeant and three men examined the Union mounts and exchanged laconic terms of Texas disgust when finding signs of inexperience-caused neglect. Born in a land where a horse was a way of life rather than a mere means of transport, they felt little but disgust for the Yankees from the industrial East, many of whom rode seriously for the first time on enlistment.

Having faith in his men, Dusty left them to their duties with the minimum of supervision. While looking around the camp, his eyes came to rest on the small civilian who still sat on the wooden box and had apparently been overlooked by the Texans. Telling Wormold to join the other

Yankee officers, Dusty turned and walked towards the small man.

"I'm a civilian, not a soldier," the man yelped as Dusty drew near. "Henry S. Oliver, clerk to the Baptist Mission For Indian Betterment."

"Some of them sure need bettering," Dusty replied. "What's in the box, Mr. Oliver?"

"Religious tracts. The Good Book translated into the heathen Cherokee tongue so that the savages too may be shown the light."

"Mind if I take a look?"

"Do officers of the Confederate States Army rob civilians and men of the church?" demanded Oliver hotly, coming to his feet and walking forward.

"If tracts are inside, they'll not be touched," Dusty promised. "Open it up, sir."

"Woe is the day when the work of the Lord shall be put down by the un-godly and His servants beset by evil-doers!" moaned Oliver. "Can't you take my word as to the contents, brother?"

"As a man, yes," Dusty replied. "But as an officer with a duty to do, I'll have to see inside the box."

"Very well, then," sighed Oliver resignedly and produced a key from his jacket pocket. "But I will not condone the Devil's work by opening it."

"See to it, Billy Jack," ordered Dusty and a faint smile flickered on his lips. "I reckon you're sinful enough for this not to make any difference."

"Happen it does," drawled the sergeant major, "I'll certain sure let you know about it."

With that, Billy Jack took the key and walked towards the box.

CHAPTER TWO

A Box Full of Confederate Money

"Hold it, Billy Jack!"

The words cracked from Dusty's lips and brought the sergeant major to an immediate halt. Turning, he looked upon his commander and waited to be told what caused the change of plans.

Almost three years of war and danger gave Dusty an instinct, or second sense which warned him of peril. Suddenly he became aware of the familiar sensations; something was wrong and he wondered what. Swiftly his mind ran through the sequence of events. He felt sure that the box contained articles more significant than mere religious tracts. If anything, Oliver spoke too glibly; and dressed wrongly for a member of an obscure church mission organisation.

When handing over the key to Billy Jack, Oliver for a moment lost his air of martyrdom. Only for a moment did it go, but during that time the man showed hate, disappointment and a little satisfaction. For some reason Oliver wanted them to undertake the actual opening of the box. In fact he had fallen back as Billy Jack approached it and stood so as to place Dusty between him and the sergeant major. All that had registered subconsciously to Dusty, triggering off his warning instincts and causing him to stop Billy Jack. Unless Dusty was sadly wrong, Billy Jack might regret opening the box should he do so.

"What's up, Cap'n Dusty?" Billy Jack asked.

"Leave it," Dusty replied. "We'll take it back unopened."

"Let me do it for you," Oliver offered, stepping by Dusty and speaking in a voice which sounded just a mite shakey.

"Stop right there!" Dusty ordered. "I'm taking it back—."

"All right," answered Oliver and shrugged his shoulders.

In doing so, he pressed his left elbow against his side in what appeared to be a casual manner. Almost immediately his cuff jerked in a peculiar manner and a Henry Deringer Pocket Pistol slid from the sleeve into his hand. Smoothly done, the move showed long practice in controlling the pistol and its holster, which was built on the same lines as a card hold-out device used by crooked gamblers. Most people would have been taken by surprise by the sudden appearance of the pistol.

Dusty Fog proved to be an exception. Back home in the Rio Hondo country, he learned gun-handling from men well-versed in all its aspects. Part of his training covered concealment of weapons and the various methods by which a hidden pistol might be produced unexpectedly yet suddenly. Fortunately he had been watching the man, or he might have missed the elbow pressure required to set the hold-out's springs working.

Seeing a danger, a lesser person might easily have panicked, drawn, cut Oliver down and possibly have created a chain-reaction of shooting among the guards over the prisoners. Despite the urgency, Dusty realised the delicate nature of the situation and refrained from using his Colt as a means of rectifying it. All too well he could see the Yankee enlisted men's reactions to the sight of a rebel officer shooting down a man of the church; as they imagined Oliver to be.

Realising that, Dusty acted accordingly. Even as he went into action, he became aware of Oliver's peculiar behaviour.

At the sight of the pistol, Billy Jack discarded his pose of lackadaisical misery and showed himself to be a bone-tough Texas fighting man. Flinging himself to one side and down, he drew his right hand Colt while dropping to the ground. It appeared that he moved so fast, he caught Oliver unprepared. Certainly the small civilian made no attempt to correct his aim and continued to line the Deringer at the box. So Billy Jack held his fire. Being all too familiar with Dusty's deadly speed, Billy Jack knew the small Texan could easily have drawn and shot Oliver. As he did not, Cap'n Dusty clearly required the man alive and Billy Jack respected his commanding officer's wants.

From where he stood, Dusty could follow the way in which Oliver lined the gun. The hesitation in following Billy Jack's diving body did not go with the smooth manner by which Oliver produced the hide-out pistol. Nor did there appear to be any point in the man shooting Billy Jack *after* the sergeant major turned away from the box. To Dusty's way of thinking, Oliver intended to hit the box—and a particular part of it at that.

Having reached that conclusion in a flickering blur of thought, Dusty set about dealing with the matter. He acted with the kind of speed that would in the future gain him the name as the fastest gun in Texas.

Out shot his hands, but he did not waste valuable time in trying to knock the gun from Oliver's grasp. Catching the man's right wrist between his hands, with the thumbs uppermost and fingers around the joint bones, Dusty pivoted to the left until standing almost with his back to and behind Oliver. Then he drew the trapped arm until it was held before him and slid his left hand along to close over the pistol-filled fist. The action caused Oliver to lose his balance and stumble. Swiftly Dusty reversed the direction of the man by stepping back a pace and twisting on the wrist. Oliver went down on to his back, but the pain caused by his wrist and the momentum of his fall caused him to turn right over and land face down. Stepping around the man's head, Dusty turned the pistol and drew it from the clutching fingers.

As Oliver went over, he let out a screech far in excess of the pain he received. At the sound Benson began to rise, hot anger showing on his young face. Seeing an apparently unprovoked attack on the little civilian, he forgot all his previous thoughts on Dusty's chivalry. An uneasy ripple of movement passed through the seated ranks of Yankee prisoners and the watching Texans hefted their weapons to a more convenient position ready for use.

"Sit still!" ordered Red Blaze, twisting his right hand palm out and drawing the off-side Colt cavalry-style, to line it on Benson.

"Do it, damn you!" snapped Wormold, alert to the danger his shavetail's behaviour threatened to create. "First sergeant, make the men stay still." Then he glared at Red. "Does the Texas Light Cavalry make a habit of assaulting civilians, Mr. Blaze?"

"Likely Dusty had good reason," Red replied loyally. "Let's wait and see, shall we?"

"We'll do that," Wormold agreed, conscious that he could do no other.

"Lemme up!" Oliver whined. "I'm through."

Releasing the man's wrists, Dusty stepped clear. Already Billy Jack had regained his feet and stood looking at Dusty, wondering what the hell was going on. Moving slowly, as if hurt by his fall, Oliver raised himself on to hands and knees. Suddenly he flung himself forward, in the direction of the box. Out shot Billy Jack's right arm, catching Oliver by the scruff of the neck as he passed and heaving him backwards. Even so, the small man lashed a kick at the box and his boot narrowly missed colliding with its lock. Then he went staggering backwards in Dusty's direction.

At the second attempt by Oliver to destroy the box—for

Dusty felt sure that lay behind the civilian's actions—the small Texan called off being gentle. As Oliver reeled towards him, Dusty struck in a certain way taught to him by his uncle, Ole Devil Hardin's personal servant. Although many people thought Tommy Okasi was Chinese, he claimed to hail from the Japanese islands. Wherever he came from originally, Tommy possesed some mighty effective fighting tricks and taught them to the smallest member of the Hardin, Fog and Blaze clan. Using the *ju-jitsu* or *karate* techniques passed to him by Tommy Okasi, Dusty could handle bigger and stronger men with comparative ease. Nor did his knowledge hinder him in dealing with Oliver.

Around lashed Dusty's right arm, the hand held open with fingers together and thumb bent across the palm. Its heel chopped hard against the base of Oliver's skull in the *tegatana,* handsword, of *karate.* While such a method looked awkward and might be judged unlikely to be effective by a man trained in Occidental fist-fighting, Dusty had no cause to complain. On receiving the blow, Oliver dropped like a head-shot rabbit and lay still.

"Hawg-tie him, Billy Jack," Dusty ordered.

"Yo!" answered the sergeant major and looked around. "Hey, Tracey Prince, bring over some rope from that centre wagon."

One of the troopers obeyed and Billy Jack swiftly secured Oliver. Dusty looked around the camp, seeing sullen resentment on Yankee faces and interest among his own men. However, the Texans still had the situation well under control and Dusty aimed to keep it that way.

"What in hell made him act that ways, Cap'n Dusty?" asked Billy Jack after completing his task.

"Damned if I know," Dusty replied. "Give me the key and I reckon I'll find out about it."

Walking to the box, Dusty circled and studied it. By all outer appearances, Oliver took a lot of trouble and considerable risk for nothing. The box was maybe three foot long, by two high and deep, made of white pine, with a built-in lock to its hinged lid. Although Dusty held the key in his hand, he did not offer to use it. Unless he missed his guess, Oliver tried first to drive a bullet into the lock and then kick it. Not to jam its mechanism, for that would delay the opening only the few minutes required to smash through the lid.

So why did Oliver chance being killed by trying to shoot at the lock?

Slowly Dusty turned the box on end and examined its sides, but he saw nothing in its design or workmanship to interest him. Then he looked at the bottom. It had a stout framework screwed firmly around its edges to hold the base on to the sides.

"Never saw a box with its bottom screwed on afore, Cap'n Dusty," commented Billy Jack, standing behind the small Texan.

"Likely there's a good reason for it," Dusty answered. "Guidon!" The company's guidon-carrier came over from where he had stood awaiting orders. "Fetch me a screw-driver from one of the wagons."

"Yo!" answered the young man who carried the Company's identifying pennant on the march, while attending to the commanding officer's mount as required.

While waiting for the screw-driver, Dusty collected Oliver's Deringer from where it lay on the ground and walked over to the Union officers' fire.

"Why d'you reckon a man of the church carried a Deringer, Captain Wormold?" he asked, showing the small pistol to them.

"You mean he tried to shoot you?" asked Wormold.

"Something like that."

"He thought you meant to rob him," suggested the first lieutenant.

"That'd be a mighty Christian way to act, mister," Dusty drawled. "Shooting a man down to save some religious tracts. Especially when I'd told him that we'd not take them were that all he carried."

"Did he know you'd keep your word?" asked the first lieutenant.

"That depends on the kind of officers he's come across on your side, mister," Dusty answered. "And remember one thing, *mister*; when he made his move, he might easy have stirred up a mess that cost damned near all your men their lives."

"But Mr. Oliver's a man of peace," Benson put in. "He'd not know the danger, Captain Fog."

"I've got the screw-driver, Cap'n," called the guidon-carrier.

"Excuse me, gentlemen," Dusty said and turned to walk back to the box.

The short talk had been a waste of time in one respect, although it enabled Dusty to clarify his position over the incident. Despite having watched carefully, he failed to detect the slightest hint that the Yankee officers knew their passenger to be other than a member of the Baptist Mission For Indian Betterment.

Taking the screw-driver, Dusty knelt by the box and went carefully to work. After removing the screws, he moved the framework and slid away the bottom board. Before his eyes lay proof that Oliver had good reason for not wanting the box open.

"Whooee!" the guidon-carrier yelped, staring down with eyes bugged out like organ stops. "I never before saw that much money in all my life."

His comment was very apt. All the interior space of the box was filled with packs of new Confederate money. While the guidon-carrier looked down and saw no more than the bare sight of the money, Dusty stared and thought. The small Texan wondered why a Yankee civilian travelling on a Union Army supply convoy would be carrying a large sum of the enemy's money.

One answer sprang to mind. The U.S. Secret Service maintained spy-rings throughout Texas, Arkansas, and the Indian Nations and its members needed rebel money for operating expenses. Most likely Oliver acted as pay-master for them. His actions earlier proved that he knew of the box's contents and sought to destroy them before they fell into the rebels' hands.

In which case Oliver became a catch of major importance. Most likely the Confederate Secret Service would be only too pleased to have in their hands a man so high among their opposite numbers that he carried payments for Yankee spies. With any amount of luck, Company 'C' ought to return to the Regiment's headquarters in time to hand over Oliver to a person who would know the best way to deal with him.

While studying the money, Dusty became aware of the apparent thickness of the box's walls. He took out three of the pads of money from level with the lock and looked into the space. It seemed that the inside of the box had been coated with a familiar-looking material. Unless Dusty missed his guess as he ran a finger over the box's lining, the material was wet-stretched pig's intestines coated with chemicals to make them inflammable and shellacked for a water-resistant finish. Self-consuming cartridges made of the same material sometimes came his way and he could not mistake the sight or touch of the lining. Nor did he feel the solid hardness of wood beneath the pig's skin, instead it gave slightly as if some softer substance separated it from the pine.

Dusty went no further with his experiments, preferring to leave the solving of the box's mystery to hands trained in such work. He put the three pads he had taken into his pocket, then telling the guidon-carrier to secure the box's base, Dusty called Red and Billy Jack to him. They saw enough of the contents to arouse their interest.

"Could be the lil feller didn't know what was inside," Billy Jack commented.

"Happen he thought it was the church funds," Red went on with a grin.

"You're a big help," Dusty answered. "This's why he tried to put a bullet into the lock."

"That wouldn't stop us opening the box for long," Red said. "We could easy bust in the lid."

"Didn't need to," Billy Jack put in. "He'd already give me the key—"

"And didn't make his move until after I'd told you to leave opening it up," Dusty pointed out. "I reckon we'll let an armourer take a look at that box."

"If you're thinking what I know you're thinking," Billy Jack said fervently. "Thanks for stopping me."

"It's my pleasure," Dusty assured him. "I'd rather have the devil I know than start getting a new sergeant major used to my ways. Get ready to pull out."

"You want the usual doing, Dusty?" asked Red.

Only for a moment did Dusty hesitate. No matter how often he did it, he could never quite reconcile himself to taking horses from his enemies.

"Do the usual," he said. "Take them all."

True to the code of the Texas range country, Dusty did not lightly set a man a-foot. An old Texas saying ran, 'A man without a horse is no man at all.' To the majority of people in the Lone Star State being set a-foot ranked as the worst possible fate and not infrequently led to the horse-less one's death.

However, Dusty accepted that he must take all the horses; not only because his Company expected it, but as part of his duty as an officer in the Confederate States Army. He knew that the loss of the supplies would have a great de-moralising effect on the Yankees—as also would his act of leaving them two-thirds of the medical supplies—and so he put aside his distaste in the interests of his duty.

Thinking of the medical supplies brought up another point and Dusty acted on it.

"Red," he said as his cousin turned to supervise the loading of the box on to a wagon. "Pick out two horses—no, mules if they have them—and leave them as a team for the ambulance."

"It'll be mules then," Red replied.

Strolling over to the officers' fire, Dusty said, "We'll be pulling out now, Captain Wormold."

"You didn't have your cup of coffee," Wormold answered, determined to prove he could accept defeat gracefully.

"I'll have it now then," Dusty smiled, glancing around him.

Already the wagons had been prepared to move, their teams hitched up by men assigned to the duty. Another party arrived with Company 'C's' horses and Billy Jack, without waiting for instructions, ordered half of the men guarding the Yankees to mount up. Everything ran with a smooth, orderly precision which allowed no opportunity for the Yankees to make a move at changing the situation. At no time were they left without armed men ready to quell any attempt at escaping or overpowering the rebels.

"You'll find your vedettes, pickets and riding patrols hawg-tied and gagged at the picket sites," Dusty remarked, sipping at the coffee.

"Are any of them injured?" Wormold demanded.

"Sore heads and rope-burned necks is all."

That gave Wormold the picture of how and why his circle of guards failed to raise the alarm. It also did nothing to lessen his admiration for the skill showed by the Texans. Stalking a lone vedette might be fairly simple, but silencing a full picket offered greater difficulty and that did not include the collection of the communicating patrols which passed constantly between the grand guard and pickets. Yet those Texans brought it off and performed most of the delicate work without any supervision from their officers. Wormold shuddered as he thought of the noiseless approach, the silent swish as ropes flew out to settle about Yankee necks, or gun butts descended to silence any Union out-cry. If the rebels were the sadistic, blood-thirsty fiends the liberal newspapers made them appear, Wormold would be burying at least half of his command the following morning instead of freeing hands and attending to minor injuries.

Sipping appreciatively at his coffee—the Union block-ade of Texas' coastline putting it among the commodities in short supply—Dusty watched the final preparations to leave. Billy Jack sent the guidon-carrier and another man to collect Oliver and carry the bound man to the wagons.

"What's this, Captain Fog?" Wormold asked.

"I'm taking Mr. Oliver along," Dusty replied.

"As a hostage?" growled the first lieutenant.

"Wake up, mister!" Dusty barked. "Oliver's carrying a box full of Confederate money. He knew what he was car-rying and it's likely for distribution to Yankee spies. So he's coming with me, mister. If our brass decide he's innocent, I'll be disciplined and he'll be returned with apologies."

Clearly the lieutenant understood the subtle differences between a harmless enemy civilian and an agent employed as pay-master and go-between for spies. If he did not, Wormold and Benson knew for they made no objections. In fact Wormold began to transfer his indignation and rage from Dusty to Oliver. No professional soldier cared for spies, although admitting they had their uses, and Wormold liked Oliver a whole lot less when considering that the man had been willing to throw away many lives to safeguard his secret.

"We understand, Captain Fog," he stated.

"Then I'll thank you for the coffee and be on my way," Dusty replied. "I'm leaving you a couple of mules to haul the ambulance."

"Thanks," Wormold answered, understanding the reason for selecting that particular kind of team. Mules could not travel at the speed of horses and one trained for harness-work showed a strenuous reluctance to being saddled for riding. While Dusty left the Yankees with the means of hauling their medical supplies, he prevented them from us-ing the animals as a way of sending for reinforcements. "You seem to have thought of everything."

"I try, Captain," Dusty smiled. "I surely try."

Looking around his denuded, disarmed, horseless camp after the sound of the rebel hooves faded into the distance, Captain Wormold decided that Dusty did far better than merely try—he made a damned good job of it.

CHAPTER THREE

A Talented Yankee Gentleman

Captain Buck Blaze looked like a slightly older, not so pugnacious version of his brother Red. However he lacked Red's genius for becoming involved in fights, which might be thought of as a blessing. Annoyance of the kind which might have sent Red off on the hunt for a brawl filled Buck as he watched the way Miss Belle Boyd stood laughing and chatting with that preacher who came on a visit from back East to the Regiment.

Not that Buck had anything against preachers, even one as well-dressed and handsome as the Reverend Julius Ludlow. Nor, if the truth be told, could Buck lay any claim to Belle's affections. What riled him was that he had escorted Belle to the ball and, until one of their host's servants brought her a note which she read, she had behaved in a perfectly correct manner. Then, for no reason at all, she had excused herself and went over to lay the full weight of her charm on Ludlow—and, mister, that was a whole load of charm to be wasted on a visiting preacher.

25

Without a doubt Belle Boyd could claim to be the most beautiful and best dressed woman attending the ball. Of course, as the other ladies present repeatedly told themselves, the horrid Yankee blockade prevented people who didn't have influential friends from obtaining the latest fashion dresses. Perfectly true, too; and it seemed that Belle possessed the necessary qualifications for beating the blockade. The dress she wore was white silk, with a light blue sash about its waist, cut on the latest Eastern lines guaranteed to attract the attention of every male and envy of each woman present.

While the other women might make catty comments about her clothes, none could fault her in the matter of looks. A tall, willowy girl—but not skinny by any means—her neatly coiffeured brunette hair framed a beautiful face with lines of intelligence and breeding on it. Small wonder that she attracted attention among the guests at the ball.

Certainly Ludlow gave no sign of wishing to leave Belle's company. After coming from the floor at the end of a spirited Virginia reel, he listened to something the girl said, nodded and escorted her towards the open doors of the big room. Several of the women exchanged glances and disapproving clucks at the sight. Buck felt his annoyance grow. Normally he did not profess to sit in judgement on other people's morals; but he felt that Belle should remember who she was and, if she wished to use a mild flirtation as a means of relaxation, should select somebody more suitable than a preacher.

Then Buck found himself wondering if there might be some deeper motive behind the girl's actions. He could hardly believe that she found the need to relax in such a manner, even after her last trip. Maybe Belle possessed some deeper reason for her interest in Ludlow. If so, she might require help. Buck could not forget the slight, but significant change which came over Belle as she read the note. Although she had a mobile face, he knew it usually showed only such emotions as she wished to have seen. On reading the note, a blank, expressionless mask momentarily replaced her friendly attitude. Then she slipped the note into her vanity bag, excused herself in the formal way which gave no real reason, and left the party of young people with whom she had been talking. Going over, she began to exert all her charm on Ludlow and, preacher or not, he showed no reluctance to be so charmed.

"Come on, Buck, don't you-all stand day-dreaming," said his identical twin brother, Pete. "The Swinton gals want for you and me to take them home after the ball."

"Huh?" grunted Buck, coming out of his reverie. "Sure, Pete."

"It's lucky for you that I didn't say give me that new hoss of yours," Pete grinned. "You're not starting to think about Belle as your gal, now are you?"

"Nope. I'm just a touch curious."

"Over why she'd go for a preacher when there's a handsome, gallant, dashing young Cavalry captain all ready to lay his fame and fortune at her dainty feet?"

"Something like that," smiled Buck. "What's she see in that feller, Pete?"

"How's that?" Pete asked.

"Take away his fancy preacher's clothes, curly brown hair, good looks and soft white hands," drawled Buck, "and what've you got?"

"You," Pete replied. "Let's go talk to the Swinton gals. If Belle's wanting a change of company, she's old enough to pick it."

"But if she knows something about that preacher—," Buck began.

"She's full capable of handling it herself," Pete finished. "All you, or I, could do is spoil things for her and that'd get her riled."

"Which same I wouldn't want to happen," drawled Buck. "Come on, Brother Pete, you're keeping me and the Swinton gals waiting."

"It's hell being born into a family of ready liars," Pete

sighed and the brothers walked across the floor.

Standing on the porch, Belle sucked in a deep breath and vigorously plied her fan.

"Lordy lord!" she said, looking at Ludlow. "Isn't it hot?"

"I'm afraid our host's house isn't large enough for his ambitions," he replied. "Inviting the General's staff and officers from the near-by Regiment as well as the local gentry does crowd everyone together."

"Could we possibly take a stroll, do you think?" Belle asked, peeking coyly over the top of her fan. "Lordy, isn't that forward of me. But I feel that if I go back inside just yet, I'll just melt right away."

"I wouldn't want that to happen," Ludlow answered and took her arm.

As they walked Belle prattled on in an empty-headed manner, sounding like the kind of rich, pampered, spoiled Southern belle portrayed on stage in the highly patriotic Yankee plays of the moment. Ludlow listened, making only such 'no' or 'yes' comments as the situation demanded. While doing so, he directed their feet towards the stables. Its doors stood open and lanterns hung inside to illuminate the interior. Edging Belle towards the doors, Ludlow peered inside to ensure that the building was unoccupied.

"And I said to Susie-Mae Swinton—," Belle continued with the pointless story she had begun when he suddenly thrust her through the doors and into the stables. Shock came to her face as she stared at the man. "Why—Why Julius Ludlow. And you-all a man of the cloth—for shame!"

"It won't work, Miss Parrish—if that's your name," Ludlow growled, moving towards her and taking what appeared to be a large, heavy key from his pocket. "I reckon you'd best drop that vanity bag."

Still maintaining her expression of fright and shock, Belle stared down at Ludlow's right hand. In it he held the key with three fingers through the ring handle, the fore-finger curled around a stud on the bar. Belle noticed that the bar of the key appeared to be hollow. While aware of what the other held, she tried a bluff.

"Just what do you think you're playing at?" she asked. "You didn't need to push me in here just to show me your old church key."

"Drop it, Miss Parrish!" Ludlow growled. "That wig fooled me at first, but you're the girl I saw fencing with Buck Blaze at the camp. And even if I hadn't seen you there, I'd know. Up until the time you came over to me, you made real intelligent conversation. What was in the note?"

"Note?"

"I saw the coon bring it to you. And I won't ask you to drop that bag again. Do it right now."

"Why I don't know what you mean," Belle insisted and slipped the bag from her fingers. "I do really think you're deranged in your head, Ju—."

"No you don't," Ludlow answered. "And you're acting wrong again. If you really thought this was only an old church key, you'd be screaming your head off for help right now."

"I always heard one should humour crazy people," Belle said, her hands plucking nervously at the dress sash.

"Keep them where I can see them!" Ludlow ordered. "This key-gun's only .36 but this close it'll kill—."

Silk rustled as the sash and skirt of Belle's dress parted company from the bodice to slide down to the ground. What it revealed, along with the unexpected nature of her action, halted Ludlow open-mouthed and staring in his tracks. Belle wore neither under-skirt nor petticoats; understandable on such a warm evening, even if the Yankee blockade did not place such items in very short supply among the Southern ladies. However instead of the usual knee-long drawers one might expect a well-bred young lady to wear, Belle stood exposed in a pair of the most daring, short-legged black under-garments Ludlow had seen on, or off, a stage. Although of slim build, Belle had shapely legs muscled like a dancer's. A dancer's, or a—

Just a shade too late Ludlow thought of another type of person who acquired such muscular development in the legs; although it must be admitted at that time very few women came into that particular class.

The instant her action distracted Ludlow, Belle moved fast. First she flicked her fan at the man's face and instinctively he brought up his right hand to protect his features. In doing so he took the key-gun out of line of the girl. Up rose her right leg, the white of the thigh flashing against the black suspender straps and black silk stockings, to drive the toe of her high-heeled calf-high boot with some force straight into Ludlow's groin.

Agony ripped into Ludlow with such severity that it caused him to double over and the gun dropped from his fingers. Nor did he find time to recover from the nauseating torment which filled him and prevented cohesive thought from warning him of danger. Bringing down her right foot from delivering the kick, Belle glided forward. No longer did her face look frightened, but held an expression of grim determination. Throwing her weight on to the right foot, Belle thrust her left leg up. Bending the left knee and pointing the toe down, she propelled it with all her strength to crash into Ludlow's offered face. The force of the attack caused Belle's knee to burst through the material of the stocking and lifted Ludlow erect. He did not stay that way for long. Drawing back her right fist, she whipped it across to collide with Ludlow's jaw. A solid click sounded and the man spun around, crashed into the side of a stall, then slid down into its straw.

None of Belle's attack gave any sign of being made by a thoroughly scared, scatter-brained girl of the kind she acted earlier. The punch whipped around with the skill and precision many a man might have envied; while the way she kicked would have done credit to any of the French-Creole *savate* fighters Ludlow had seen in New Orleans.

Blowing on her stinging knuckles, Belle worked the fingers and looked in Ludlow's direction. Unless she missed her guess, he would not be troubling her for at least a couple of minutes. So she decided to make herself more presentable. If any of the guests should happen to come to the stables, her state of undress would call for more explanation than she cared to give.

Taking up her sash and skirt, she gave them a shake to remove any traces of their contact with the ground. After donning the skirt, she took up her vanity bag and the key-pistol. Slowly she turned the latter over in her hands, making sure that she kept the barrel pointing away from her. Although Belle knew of such things, the pistol she held was the first of its kind to come into her hands.

From what Belle could see, the pistol had been well made. Its outer surfaces showed the dull, rust-pitted appearance one expected from the main key of an old church. The inside of the barrel had the clean, shining glint of new metal. Most likely it incorporated some kind of easily removable barrel-cap when not in use to prevent its true purpose being detected. She would know when they searched Ludlow.

Originally such pistols had been designed for use by jailers, serving to open the cell doors and provide an instantly available weapon should a prisoner try an attack. Belle knew the one she held must be of more modern construction and wondered how it worked. It might make use of the metallic cartridges becoming so popular among the Yankees; or take a charge of loose powder, ignited by a percussion cap, to fire its bullet. Although curious to learn, Belle knew better than to experiment. The time might come when she could use such a device, but she preferred to allow a trained gunsmith to learn how it operated.

Hearing footsteps approaching the stables, Belle dropped the pistol into her bag. She glanced again at Ludlow, seeing no sign of recovery, and moved towards the door. From the poor quality of his clothing, the man who approached her did not attend the ball as a guest. He was big, well-built, yet looked neither slow nor awkward. Studying the man, Belle concluded it might be unwise to try *savate* on him should he be an enemy. Given the element of surprise, she might be able to render him helpless. If she failed, he looked strong enough to half kill her.

So Belle slipped her right hand casually into the mouth of her bag. Ignoring the key-pistol, as she was unsure how to work it, the girl eased her fingers through the bracelet which rested in a pouch stitched to the side of the bag. She moved carefully, for the bracelet had a razor-sharp edge for use in emergencies.

"Southrons, hear your country call you," the man said quietly.

On hearing the first line of the militantly patriotic words General Albert Pike put to Daniel B. Emmet's song "Dixie," Belle relaxed. The Confederate Secret Service used it as a password by which agents could identify themselves to each other. Satisfied that there would be no danger, Belle still retained her hold of the bracelet. In its way, that bracelet was every bit as much a weapon as the key-pistol and no more likely to be suspected.

"Up lest worse than death befall you," she replied, giving the counter-sign.

"Absom sent me, the name's Tolling," the man said, entering the barn and looking her over with approval. "So you're Miss Boyd. It's a honour to meet up with you, ma'am."

"I hope I'm not too much of a disappointment," Belle smiled.

Despite her light answer, Belle felt pleased with the man's obvious pleasure. It had been a hard struggle in the early days to gain male approval and acceptance by the Confederate States Secret Service, but now she was firmly established and shared honours with Rose Greenhow as the leading female lights of that organisation. Between them, the two young women extracted much information and caused the Yankees untold trouble.

In an age when young women of good birth were expected to be fragile, sheltered creatures, Belle received almost a unique upbringing. Born into a wealthy Southern family, she grew up with every advantage and luxury. However her father tended to be eccentric in some ways and made up for the disappointment of not having a son by teaching the girl to ride, handle a gun and other male accomplishments. A talented girl, Belle learned from her father without losing any of her femininity or forgetting to gain skill in female matters.

When the Civil War first began to rear its head in the distance, Belle's father stood out for the right of any sovereign state to secede from the Union if its interests clashed with the Federal Government; one of the main causes of the War, although the Yankees made much use of the slavery issue as being more likely to induce the masses to fight. Some weeks before the commencement of actual hostilities, a bunch of Union supporters attacked Belle's home. They killed her mother and father, wounding the girl and might have done worse if the family's "downtrodden and abused" slaves had not arrived and driven off their "saviours." By the time she recovered, the War had begun. Belle put her increased hatred of the Yankees to good use. Joining her cousin, Rose Greenhow, she became an agent for the Confederate Secret Service, often delivering the information gathered personally. Stonewall Jackson himself referred to Belle as his best courier, after she brought news to him which helped make possible the victory at the first battle of Bull Run.

Since then Belle carried on the good work. While the Yankees knew her name, skilled use of disguises prevented her from being recognised. Pinkerton, soon to form his own detective agency, had his best operatives after Belle but without success.

Using information she gathered, Belle had recently completed an assignment. With Dusty Fog's aid, she captured a Yankee Army payroll and used the money to buy arms for the South.* Resting until orders arrived directing her to another assignment, she posed as one of General Ole Devil Hardin's kin on a visit from Texas. As such she naturally received an invitation to the ball. On receiving Tolling's message that Ludlow was not all he seemed, Belle forgot relaxation and went into action with all the deadly efficiency that gained her the name "the Rebel Spy."

"Absom said you had black hair," Tolling remarked as they walked across to and looked down at the groaning, stirring man.

"This is a wig," Belle replied, touching her 'hair.' Your note didn't say much about him. Who is he?"

"His real name's Byron and he's a real talented Yankee gentleman."

"One of their spies?"

"Paid by them for it, anyways."

"And his game?"

"Afore the War he used to work the riverboats," Tolling explained. "Making up to rich women, cheating at cards. Got him a way of becoming real friendly."

"And now?"

"There you've got me. He's one of a bunch who the Yankees sent out of New Orleans. Lucienne got on to them and sent me after him. Only he travelled faster'n me and I've only just caught up with him."

"We'll have to see if we can make him talk," the girl remarked. "Only we can't do it here or now. Can you keep him hidden until I find help to take him away?"

"I reckon so," Tolling drawled. "Only he'll likely make a fuss when he comes to. If he does, I'll whomp him over the head."

"You might do it too hard," the girl smiled. "They do say Yankees have soft skulls. I've a better way, if you fetch me some water."

Crossing the stable to a pump fitted on to a stone sink

Told in "The Colt and the Sabre."

in one corner, Tolling took up the metal dipper which hung on its side. He worked the pump's handle, filled the dipper with water and returned to the girl. In his absence she had taken a ring with a large, heavy stone set into it from her bag. Holding the ring over the dipper, she touched its side and the stone flicked upwards at one side from the setting. A brown powder trickled out of the cavity exposed beneath the raised stone, dribbling into the water where it dissolved without a visible trace.

"That's neat," Tolling said as the girl pressed the stone back into place.

"Rose Greenhow suggested it and had one made for each of us," Belle replied. "Although I think she stole the idea from reading about the Borgia family in Italy. If he drinks that he'll give you no trouble."

"He'll drink it," Tolling assured her.

Although they both were prepared to deal with some reluctance on Ludlow's part, it failed to materialise. Most likely he would have objected to accepting a drink if he retained his normal quick wits. However Belle's treatment robbed him of them temporarily and pain gave him a thirst. So he drank greedily when Tolling held the dipper to his lips.

"He's taking it like a deacon at a whisky still," grinned Tolling.

Hearing the voice, Ludlow focused his eyes first on the speaker, then past Tolling to where Belle stood. With a low curse, Ludlow tried to force himself up from the floor.

"Don't worry," Belle told Tolling as he reached down to restrain Ludlow.

Before Ludlow could do more than haul himself into a sitting position, the powder took effect. His body went limp and he slipped down to the floor again. Bending down, Tolling made a quick investigation and straightened up with a satisfied nod of his head.

"He's sleeping like a babe, Miss Boyd. That's real potent stuff. What is it?"

"I never learned its name," the girl replied. "Rose got a supply of it from the clerk of a river-boat. He claimed that a small dose would put the biggest man to sleep and keep him that way for a couple of hours; and it does."

At that moment they heard the drumming of rapidly approaching hooves. Telling her companion to hide Ludlow under the straw, Belle darted to the stable door and looked out. A sigh of relief came from her as she recognised the rider who came towards her. If anything, she would find the problem of secretly removing Ludlow made easier with the newcomer's arrival.

CHAPTER FOUR

A Fortune in Counterfeit Money

"Why Cousin Dusty," Belle greeted, walking towards the small Texan as he halted his horse. "I surely didn't expect to see you back here so soon."

For a moment the brunette wig fooled Dusty, then recognition came and he wondered what Belle might be doing at the stables.

"I only just got in," he replied, swinging from the saddle. "Was told back to the Regiment that Uncle Devil's here and so I came right over. Is he up to the house, Belle?"

"He surely is," Belle agreed, speaking as she had all the time in the world for she saw a young officer approaching them. "I just knew something would happen to spoil his evening. 'Beulah Parrish!' I said when I saw you coming, 'Cousin Dusty's bringing trouble for Uncle Devil for certain sure.'"

"You could be right at that, Cousin Beulah," Dusty drawled, grinning inwardly at the neat way in which Belle passed on her current identity. "Only it's nothing to spoil his night."

Catching Dusty's head shake, the officer steered his companion by without doing more than call a greeting. One look at Dusty's appearance told Belle that he had ridden long and hard. So she put aside her thoughts of asking him to help with removing Ludlow. Only a matter of some importance would bring Dusty to interrupt Ole Devil at the ball. With that in mind she reverted to her original idea of going to Buck Blaze for help.

"Why not let Tolling tend to stabling your horse?" she suggested.

"Who?"

"He works here," smiled the girl. "It will save time, Dusty."

Normally Dusty would not have thought to allow a stranger to take care of his horse, so he realised the girl must have good reason for making the suggestion. Looking to where Tolling came from the stable, Dusty noticed the man walked with a pronounced limp. All too well Tolling knew of the deserter problem which plagued both sides throughout the War. Figuring that a healthy man employed in such a menial capacity might otherwise arouse comment, Tolling adopted a means of showing why he apparently did not serve his country.

"Let me have your reins, Cap'n," Tolling offered. "I'll see to it for you."

Before leaving the horse, Dusty took three pads of money from its saddle-pouches and slipped them into the front of his tunic. Tolling led the horse away and Dusty turned to Belle.

"I'd as soon not go into the ballroom dressed like this," he said. "Reckon you can fix it for Uncle Devil to meet me outside?"

"I'll see to it," she promised. "Go around the right side of the house and wait by the first door. I'll ask the General to meet you there."

On entering the main room, Belle passed with leisurely-seeming speed to where Ole Devil sat talking to their host.

Catching the girl's slight signal, the General rose to his feet and joined her. Tall, lean, immaculate in his full-dress uniform, Ole Devil had a sharp, tanned, hawk-like face set in disciplined lines that rarely showed the true, generous nature underneath the hard exterior. When he heard of Dusty's arrival, he nodded and returned to the host. As Belle expected, Joe Hemming, their host, put his study at Ole Devil's disposal and she told the General that Dusty would be waiting at its outside door. So casually had both she and Ole Devil acted that none of the guests suspected anything might be wrong. After Ole Devil strolled off in the direction of the study, Buck Blaze drifted to Belle's side.

"You didn't have to slap that preacher's face, now did you, Cousin Beulah?" he asked with a grin.

"How'd you guess?" she replied. "I need your help, Buck."

"It's yours. What's up?"

"I'll tell you on the way to the stables," Belle promised. "Only let's make it look natural, so nobody guesses something's wrong."

Letting Dusty into Hemming's study, Ole Devil walked across to the desk, waved the youngster into a chair and sat down facing him.

"Well, Dustine," the General said. "What brings you here?"

"I'm not sure, sir," Dusty answered, taking the money from his tunic and placing it upon the desk before his uncle. "I just thought you'd be interested in this money."

"Why?" asked Ole Devil, picking up one of the bundles.

"We captured a Yankee convoy and found a box full of Confederate money in the possession of a civilian."

While Dusty spoke, Ole Devil thumbed through the notes. Then the General gave them a closer examination. When he raised his face to look at Dusty, the small Texan read interest and concern where most people could have seen no change of expression.

"A box full like this?" the General said.

"Yes, sir. I thought that the man might be taking it to the Indian Nations so he could have it passed to Yankee spies in Texas. Figured you'd be interested and as soon as we crossed the Ouachita I had the box loaded on a pack horse and came ahead of the company. They told me where to find you at Headquarters."

"The patrol went well?"

"Easy enough, sir. We hit the Yankee guard on Elk Crossing at sundown, ran them off without loss to us. There was only a half company of Stedloe's Zouaves and the Arkansas Rifles on our side gave us covering fire."

"Go fetch Miss Boyd," Ole Devil ordered when Dusty finished speaking.

Something in the General's brusque manner told Dusty that he made the correct decision in coming ahead of his Company and interrupting Ole Devil's relaxation. After the youngster left the room, Ole Devil remained seated at the desk and took up the other packets of money. Although his tanned face showed little or nothing, Ole Devil had never been more concerned than at that moment.

While walking towards the barn, Dusty wondered what caused Ole Devil's anxiety. Few people would have read the General's moods, but Dusty knew his uncle felt deep concern at the find. More than the mere capture of a Yankee spies' pay-master warranted on the surface. Ahead of Dusty, the man Belle had called Tolling emerged from the stables.

Hearing Dusty's approaching footsteps, Tolling quickly reverted to his painful-appearing limp; but suddenly realised that he had made a mistake. Not that it would matter under the circumstances; and he would never have made such a blunder in enemy territory. Anyway, Tolling mused, that small young captain—Belle had not thought to mention Dusty's identity—was unlikely to notice—

Even as the thought began to form, Tolling saw Dusty's right hand make a move. Then the man stared into the muzzle of the Army Colt which a mere three-quarters of a second before reposed harmlessly in the small Texan's left holster.

"Where'd you get the wound, *hombre?*" Dusty asked.

"At Antietam with the Hampton Legion, cap'n," Tolling answered, staring at the Colt like a snake-mesmerized cottontail rabbit.

Belle came from the stables, wondering to whom Tolling spoke. Halting, she looked from Dusty to Tolling.

"What's going on?" she said.

"Did you see the way this gent limps?" asked Dusty.

"Yes," smiled the girl. "It looked very bad."

"*Real* bad," drawled Dusty dryly. "Only it doesn't stay in the one leg."

"It's all right, Dusty," Belle chuckled. "I can vouch for Tolling."

"He's one of your crowd, is he?"

"Yes."

"Sorry, mister," Dusty said, holstering the Colt. "I figured you to be a deserter and reckoned the time to ask about it was after I made sure you couldn't argue about answering."

"You made sure of that," admitted Tolling. "I've never seen a gun come out so fast."

"I thought so too, the first time I saw it," smiled Belle and looked at Dusty. "Your business with Ole Devil didn't take long."

"He wants to see you as soon as convenient, Belle," Dusty answered.

"Which means right now, even though it's not convenient," the girl said. "Can you and Buck tend to things here, Tolling?"

"I reckon so," the man replied.

"Then I'll come straight away, Dusty," the girl stated.

Leaving the removal of Ludlow to Buck and Tolling, Belle accompanied Dusty to where Ole Devil waited for them. After seating the girl with his usual courtesy, Ole

Devil told Dusty to go through the full story of the convoy's capture again. Belle realised that something of importance lay behind the order and listened intently. Certainly Ole Devil would not call her in merely to hear the story of a successful raid.

"What do you think, Miss Boyd?" asked the General when Dusty finished.

"The box would have had an infernal contrivance fitted to destroy its contents if they were important," the girl replied. "Which a shipment of money to pay their spies would be."

"And the money itself?"

"May I see some of it, General?"

"Help yourself," authorised Ole Devil, waving a hand to the three pads of notes on the desk top.

Taking one pad up, the girl studied the top note and then turned her eyes in Dusty's direction. "They were all new notes, Dusty?"

"All I saw, although I didn't take them all out to check."

Around Belle's neck hung a pendant with a large locket attached. Reaching up, the girl unclipped the pendant and removed it. Watched by the two men, she then eased off the glass cover of the locket. Drawing the top bill from one of the pads, she held the glass over it. From where he stood, Dusty could see that the glass was in reality a powerful lens and the girl used its power of magnification to examine the bill carefully.

"Well, Miss Boyd?" asked Ole Devil.

"How big was the box you took, Dusty?" the girl inquired, ignoring the question.

"About so big," replied Dusty, demonstrating with his hands. "There'd be a fortune in it."

"And unless I'm mistaken," Belle said quietly, "it's a fortune in counterfeit money."

"Counterfeit?" Dusty repeated.

"You thought so too, General," Belle commented.

"I thought so," Ole Devil admitted.

"Likely printing their own's the only way the Yankees can lay hands on enough of our money to supply their spies, sir," Dusty remarked.

"It cuts deeper than that, Dusty," Belle put in. "Much deeper."

"Howd' you mean, Belle?"

"The Yankees could have found a mighty smart way to win the War."

"Miss Boyd's right, Dustine," Ole Devil went on. "If enough of this counterfeit money is put into circulation, it will ruin the South's economy."

"One box full, sir?" asked Dusty.

"The Yankees won't stop at just the one," Ole Devil replied and went on to explain how paper money only retained its value when its issuer possessed sufficient assets to cover its nominal value. "So if the Yankees can flood the South with this stuff they're printing, we won't be able to do so. Our economy will be smashed and that will end the War just as surely as if they whipped us on every battlefield."

"Which same they'll have to be stopped, sir," Dusty stated. "Only I'll be damned if I can see how to do it."

"The only way to do it would be to smash their printing plates and press," Belle said. "And to do that we'd have to learn where it is."

"Oliver might know," Dusty told her.

"He may," agreed Belle. "In fact he probably does. But a man fanatical enough to try to destroy that box at the cost of his own life won't talk easily."

"Even if he does, the chances are that the press'll be somewhere that we can't reach," Ole Devil pointed out.

"When will he be getting here, Dusty," asked Belle.

"Noon tomorrow at the earliest."

"I'll see him when he comes—and don't tell me that it's not a chore for a woman, please."

"It's not," snorted Ole Devil. "But then, neither is spying—but you're still the best spy we have."

"Don't let Rose Greenhow hear you say that, General,"

warned Belle with a smile. Then she became serious again. "Dusty, did Oliver mention what he was doing travelling on a Yankee convoy?"

"Going into the Indian Nations to preach to the Indians," Dusty replied.

"And so was Ludlow," Ole Devil put in.

"So Mrs. Hemming told me," the girl breathed. "Is there any chance of our leaving soon, General?"

"Certainly."

"If I can, I'd like to be around when Ludlow recovers," the girl said. "He may know something and if he does, I might be able to make him talk."

"Do you think he's involved in this business?"

"I don't know, General. But he was one of a party who left New Orleans and scattered through the South. A man like him, smooth, with a way of charming people, could go anywhere and pass the money without arousing suspicion."

"You're right at that. He came with what seemed perfectly legitimate letters of introduction."

"Give Pinkerton and the U.S. Secret Service their due, General," Belle said. "They're thorough. They'd see that he came ready to get co-operation from you and the civil authorities too."

"What do you want to do then?" Ole Devil inquired.

"Question Ludlow first. According to Tolling, he's working for the Yankees for money and that kind break easier than somebody who's doing it out of loyalty or for his beliefs. As I said, I'd like to be on hand when he recovers."

"We can pull out in ten-fifteen minutes without arousing too much comment," the General told her. "Will that do?"

"Yes. It will give me time to change and make my arrangements after we reach the camp," Belle replied.

"Shall I ride out now, sir?" Dusty asked. "If folks see me here in these clothes, they'll start wondering what brought me back and tie it in with your leaving the ball."

"Go ahead, Dustine," Ole Devil confirmed. "Where's that box of money?"

"Locked in your office, with a guard at the door and window."

"Good. Have the armourer on hand ready for when I return."

"Could you leave the box intact, General?" Belle put in. "At least until after I've seen Ludlow."

"Certainly," the General promised. "Get moving, Dustine. I'll be along with Miss Boyd and my staff as soon as I can arrange it."

Saluting, Dusty left the room. He went along to the stables and collected his horse. There was no sign of Tolling, so Dusty concluded he and Buck Blaze had already left with their prisoner. After saddling his horse, Dusty rode away from the Hemming house in the direction of the Texas Light Cavalry's camp. On the way he caught up to his cousin and Tolling as they rode in the same direction, with Ludlow hanging limply across the saddle of a third horse. Pausing long enough to learn where they intended to place the man on their arrival, Dusty pushed on again at a faster pace than the others for he had things to do at the camp.

By the time Ole Devil arrived, Dusty and the armourer were waiting in his office. On the desk stood the wooden box, untouched since being brought into the room for safe keeping. Crossing the room, Ole Devil looked down at the box and took its key which lay on the lid.

"I wouldn't do that, General," the armourer warned quietly.

"And I didn't aim to," Ole Devil replied. "What kind of infernal contrivance're they using?"

The term 'booby-trap' had not yet come into use, but such things were made and employed by the Secret Services of both sides. As a soldier, Ole Devil did not fully approve of infernal devices; although he granted that they did on occasion have their uses.

"Haven't looked too close, sir," the armourer drawled, walking to the desk. "But from what Cap'n Fog tells me, I'd say the lock's a fake. Instead of works, there'll be a couple of percussion caps inside. So when somebody puts the key in and turns it, they pop a cap and fire off a charge. Only I can't say for sure until after I've had a chance to look real close."

"If you'll wait in the next room, you'll maybe have your chance to find out for sure," Ole Devil told him. "I'll send when I need you."

"Yo!" answered the armourer, saluting and marching from the room.

"Miss Boyd will be along soon, Dustine," the General said as the door closed. "This's a serious business and I'd best see about notifying our Government so they can take precautions."

"Yes, sir," Dusty replied.

Taking up pen and paper, Ole Devil lapsed into silence and Dusty settled down to watch his uncle composing a concise report that could be passed in code over the telegraph wires to the Confederate Government. In addition the General would send a letter by courier to be passed East and give a fuller account of the affair. For a time the only sound in the room was the scratching of Ole Devil's pen. Then a knock came at the door. Rising, Dusty crossed the room. On opening the door, he found Belle outside and did not hesitate to let her enter.

No longer did Belle look the elegant Southern lady who attended the ball. In fact her appearance, as usual when clad in such a manner, drew a disapproving glance from Ole Devil. While the General reconciled himself to the girl making a success of the distasteful business of spying, he did not approve of her wearing her present kind of clothing.

With the wig removed, Belle proved to have deep black hair cut very short all round her skull. Instead of the ball gown, she wore a man's black shirt, riding breeches and boots; the shirt and breeches being tight enough to show off her slender figure to its best advantage and dispel any doubts as to her sex. Around her waist hung a gunbelt with an ivory-handled Dance Bros. .36 revolver—a Confederate copy of the 1851 Navy Colt—riding butt forward in the holster at her left side. Although it looked slightly incongruous taken with her clothes and appearance, she carried a lady's parasol in her left hand.

"We'll soon be ready, General," she remarked. "I've seen Tolling and he's prepared everything for me."

"Can we do anything for you, Miss Boyd?" Ole Devil asked, eyeing the girl's clothing in a frosty manner.

"I'd like Dusty's help during the questioning."

"Is that necessary? I don't want my officers getting a name for torturing prisoners."

"It will help me to have him along," Belle answered.

"I'm game to go along, sir," Dusty put in.

"Very well," Ole Devil growled. "Go. But this affair is not official in any way, you understand."

"Yes, sir," Dusty replied.

"There's one thing, Dusty," Belle said quietly. "If you come, you'll be under my orders. Do whatever I tell you without question and don't interfere with anything I do."

Watching the set, grim lines on the girl's face, Dusty found himself feeling almost sorry for Ludlow. He knew that Belle regarded the situation as being of vital importance and would brook no interference with her handling of the Yankee spy. Yet he also guessed that the girl would not employ crude torture methods until all other means failed. Dusty felt that watching Belle in action might be both interesting and instructive. So he nodded his agreement and then listened to what she wanted him to do.

CHAPTER FIVE

The Art of Gentle Persuasion

Sitting up on the bed, Ludlow blinked as the light from the lantern hung overhead dazzled him. He groaned as he swung his feet to the floor and clutched at his throbbing, aching head while fighting down the nausea filling his body. Slowly the throbbing and nausea died away and his dizziness ended, allowing him to take an interest in his surroundings.

He found himself in a small, stoutly-made one-room log cabin that had a small barred window in one wall faced at the other side by a door with a covered peep-hole cut into it. Significantly to Ludlow's mind, the door did not have a keyhole or latch in it. For furnishings the cabin held a bed, foot-locker, table and chair, all securely bolted to the floor. At first he could not imagine where he might be, then he realised that the cabin must be one used to hold captured Yankee officers before passing them on to a permanent prisoner-of-war camp. Securing the furnishings prevented them being used as weapons or a means of breaking down the door.

Even as Ludlow thought of that, pain bit into him and caused his hands to reach for the place where Belle kicked him. Recollection flooded back to him. Shock and fear creased his handsome face as his hands darted up to feel at his jaw. Staring wildly around the room, his eyes came to rest on a mirror hanging upon one wall. Rising from the bed, he lurched hurriedly across the room and studied his reflection in the shining steel surface.

"Thank God!" he croaked as he found that the swelling would have no permanent effect and leave no trace to disfigure his handsome features.

Before the thought that he might never again need his good looks as a means of making a living struck him, he heard the door's lock click and turned to see who entered. At first he barely recognised Belle without the wig and wearing male clothes. For all that, something told him that she, the burly civilian and small cavalry captain did not come merely to inquire about the state of his health.

"Go and sit at the table!" Belle ordered, standing with the parasol held lightly in both hands.

Seeing the futility of resistance, Ludlow crossed to the table and slid into the chair.

"What's the game?" he asked, sounding more than a shade uneasy.

"Lay your hands palm down on the table top in front of you," the girl said as if she did not hear a word he spoke.

Once again Ludlow obeyed, noticing that each of the male newcomers held lengths of rope in his hands. Giving Ludlow no chance to raise objections, Dusty and Tolling converged on him and grabbed a wrist. Fastening one of the pieces of rope around the wrist he held, Dusty drew its other end down to be secured to the top of the table leg farthest away from the prisoner. Moving no less deftly, Tolling tied Ludlow's other wrist in the same manner. Then, while Dusty secured Ludlow's arms further by fastening a rope from elbow to elbow, Tolling roped the man's legs to the chair. By the time they had finished, Ludlow sat held immobile and stared at them with growing concern.

"Now we're all set to have a little talk," Belle said.

"I don't know what you're playing at—," Ludlow began and looked at Dusty. "When General—."

"Don't look at Captain Fog!" Belle shouted. "I'm talking to you!"

"Maybe he don't reckon that a woman should be questioning him, Miss Boyd," Tolling put in.

"B-Boyd!" gasped Ludlow and stared at the girl. "So you're the Rebel Spy!"

"That's right, you stinking traitor," Belle replied, twisting at the handle of her parasol. "I'm the Rebel Spy and you're going to answer questions for me."

With that she drew the handle from the body of the parasol. Putting the lower section aside, she turned once more to face Ludlow. Instead of a piece of feminine frippery, she now held a deadly and sinister weapon. Dusty had noticed earlier that the parasol's handle appeared to be thicker than usual, but gave the matter no thought. Like Ludlow, he studied the thing Belle held and understood the need for the unfeminine thickness. Gripping the steel ball exposed by removing the parasol's upper section, Belle gave it a tug. Out slid a length of steel-coil spring and telescoped inside it was a foot of tubular steel connected to the ball.

Up and down flicked Belle's right hand and the coil-spring sent the steel rod whipping towards the table top with a force out of all proportion to her movement. A savage crack sounded as the metal ball struck the table and buried itself to half its depth in the wood less than an inch from Ludlow's right hand. Giving a startled, frightened yelp, he tried to jerk his hand away but the rope prevented him from doing so.

"How did this filth use to earn his living, Mr. Tolling?" asked the girl.

"Cheating at cards—," Tolling began.

"A man needs supple hands for that," Belle purred. "Look at them, Tolling. Those hands have been cared for, kept soft and fancy. If they were broken—."

Again the wicked spring-powered billy snapped out, crashing into the wood ever closer to Ludlow's hand. Sweat broke on to his forehead and fear twisted at his face. That a beautiful and sensual woman handled the billy made its effect so much worse. When Ludlow saw her remove the parasol handle, he expected to see it contain a knife-blade. Instead it held a far more terrifying device, for Ludlow did not doubt that the girl intended to use it against him. The steel ball would rip and smash his hands so that no doctor could repair the damage.

"You're a soldier!" he screeched, staring with terrified eyes at Dusty. "You can't let her torture me."

Again the billy whipped up and drove its ball into the table top. Dusty ran his tongue tip across dry lips as he saw the grim determination on Belle's face.

"Belle—."

"Keep quiet, Captain Fog!" Belle snapped. "I hold rank of colonel and I'm giving you a direct order. You came here at my request. So leave me to handle things my way."

While Dusty knew the girl spoke the truth about her honorary rank—given to put her in a position of authority when dealing with members of the Confederate armed forces—she had never made use of it in his presence before. Yet he knew she would not hesitate to invoke the full powers her rank gave if he interfered. So he stiffened into a brace and kept silent. Ludlow slumped in his chair as he realised that he could expect no further help from that source.

"Start talking, Byron!" Belle snapped after a brief pause to allow the full sense of his helplessness to fill the prisoner.

"I've not—," Ludlow began, then realised what name she used. "Who told you my name?"

"A man called Oliver," Belle answered, but saw no hint that Ludlow knew the name.

"And Gilpin sold you out to save his own neck back in New Orleans," Tolling went on when he saw Ludlow's negative response.

For a moment recognition flickered on Ludlow's face, showing that the name Tolling gave meant something to him. However he kept his mouth shut, wanting time to think how he might profit from his position and knowledge.

"You said the filth used to charm women, then bleed them by blackmail," Belle said gently. "He's handsome enough to do it, too."

With that she swung the billy sideways and its ball lashed at Ludlow's head. For a moment Dusty thought that the girl had struck the man's face. He heard Ludlow cry out and expected to see blood gushing from a wound. None flowed. Apparently the blow missed, but not by much.

Ludlow had felt the wind of the billy's passing and in his over-wrought state imagined that the metal ball grazed his skin. Far worse than the threat of mangled hands, to his way of thinking, would be the disfigurement of his face. Not only did his handsome features bring in money, but he prided himself on his looks. All too well he could imagine the horror in which the billy would leave him. An intelligent man, he possessed sufficient imagination to picture the work of the steel ball as it tore his features to a bloody, barely human ruin. Nor did he doubt that Belle meant to carry out her threat. The Rebel Spy had plenty of good reasons to hate Yankee spies and her abhorrence of Southern-born traitors would hardly be less.

"Talk, man. Why be ruined," Tolling said. "Gilpin sold you down the river quick enough to save his own hide."

Although Tolling lied on the matter, Ludlow did not doubt his story. Being an unprincipled rogue himself, Ludlow could not imagine other men acting differently than he would under a set of circumstances. So he accepted the lie that Gilpin, who died without talking, betrayed him. For all that, he hesitated to talk and hoped for time to think how he might put his information to the best use.

"I don't know much!" he stated hurriedly as Belle's lips tightened. "They told me to come out here, make my way across to the Indian Nations and meet one of their people in the Choctaw Indians' main village."

"And that's all you know?" Belle asked.

"That's all I know," agreed Ludlow.

"Bring in that box, gentlemen," the girl ordered.

"Sure, Miss Boyd," Tolling answered and left the room followed by Dusty.

"Captain Fog captured a Yankee agent on his way to the Choctaw village," Belle explained to Ludlow. "Maybe his property will tell us something of your mission."

Watching the man, Belle noticed him give a shocked start as he saw the box Dusty and Tolling carried in. She drew the key from her pocket as the men set the box down before Ludlow, placing it between his hands on the table. Fear flickered across Ludlow's face as she walked forward. Then his features set into hard lines. Realising that he stood a good chance of dying, Ludlow found some comfort in the fact that the girl who humiliated and captured him would also be killed. Anger at Belle for out-smarting him overrode his knowledge of what would happen when she inserted and turned the key.

"Hold it, Miss Boyd!" Tolling said urgently, just before the key entered the lock. "There may be an infernal contrivance in the keyhole."

"That's true enough," the girl admitted and stepped back. "Could you break the lock with a bullet from outside the room, Dusty?"

"Easy enough," Dusty replied.

"Then we'll go outside and watch you do it."

Although Belle, Tolling and Dusty retired from the cabin, they left Ludlow inside. Desperately he strained at his bonds, but the ropes held firm. Out in the open, at the far edge of the door's light, Belle and Tolling stood watching as Dusty took out his right side revolver then aimed in the direction of the box. If any member of Company "C" had been watching, they might have felt surprise that Dusty took so long in his aiming at a target.

Sweat began to trickle down Ludlow's face as he realised that he, and he alone, would be caught in the raging inferno when the bullet struck the box's lock. While reconciled to dying as long as Belle went with him, he did not relish meeting his end in such a manner when she stood in safety.

"Don't shoot!" he screeched. "Don't shoot. I've something to tell you."

"Hold your fire, Dusty," Belle said and walked back into the cabin. Halting, she looked down at the man. "All right, Ludlow, what is it?"

"That box'll explode if you put a bullet into it."

"We'd an idea it might."

"I can tell you how to get into it without getting killed."

"So can the armourer here in camp," sniffed the girl. "Anyway, there's nothing of importance in it, I'll bet."

"You'd be wrong!" Ludlow growled. "It's full of counterfeit Confederate money."

"How do you know that?" Belle asked.

"What's in it if I talk?"

"What do you want?"

"My life," Ludlow said simply. "I know what'll happen to me if you send me for trial. It'll be a rope, or firing squad, and I'm not wanting to die."

Belle watched the man and knew that she had won. After placing Ludlow in the cabin, Tolling and Buck Blaze had removed some of the chinking—mud packed between the logs and allowed to harden there so as to keep out draughts— and made a hole large enough for them to keep him under observation from outside. Using the vantage point, Belle had studied the man on his recovery. She noted his concern for his face and based her subsequent actions on what she saw. First she played on his fears of hand-damage and disfigurement to weaken his resistance and then brought in the box on the odd chance that he might recognise it and be aware of its contents. Without the first shock treatment, he might have hidden his knowledge; but in his disturbed state failed to do so. Unless the girl missed her guess, Ludlow meant to tell all he knew. She hoped the time spent would prove worth the effort.

"Go ahead," she ordered.

Instead of answering the girl, Ludlow looked at Dusty. "I want your word as a Confederate officer that I'll not stand trial if I talk."

"Isn't *my* word good enough?" smiled Belle.

"I don't trust any of you Secret Service bunch on either side," Ludlow told the girl and turned to Dusty. "How about it, Captain?"

"I'll do all I can for you, *if* Miss Boyd says your information's worth it."

"That's not good enough. I want your assurance that I won't have to stand trial if I talk."

"These're three bars on my collar, mister, not three stars in a laurel wreath.* I don't have authority to make that kind of agreement."

"But I do," put in Ole Devil's voice and he entered. "Sorry to butt in, Miss Boyd, but I've been watching through that hole you had made in the wall. I always wanted to see some of you Secret Service crowd using 'gentle persuasion.'"

"I suppose that General Hardin's word is good enough for you?" asked Belle.

Only for a moment did Ludlow hesitate. All too well he knew the iron code by which the true Southern gentlemen lived. If Ole Devil gave his word, he would stick by it. No matter that the people present would say nothing should he fail to do so, the General could be relied on not to go back upon his given word. As the Commanding General of the highly-successful Army of Arkansas, Ole Devil wielded considerable influence. Not even the leaders of the powerful Confederate States' Secret Service could countermand his

---

Three stars in laurel wreath: Confederate General's collar insignia.

orders. Nor would the South's Government attempt to interfere with any decision he made.

"Your word's good enough, General," Ludlow stated.

"You have it then. If, in Miss Boyd's opinion, your information has sufficient value, I give you my word that you won't stand trial for your actions."

While that placed a whole lot in Belle's hands, Ludlow realised he was in no position to argue.

"All right then," he said. "The box's full of counterfeit money—."

"You'll need to give us a whole heap more than that," Belle warned him.

"The Yankees plan to ruin the South with it!"

"With one box full?" snorted the girl. "Don't waste our time, man."

"They've more than one box full. This's only the start, Miss Boyd. They're printing more and plan to flood the South with so much counterfeit money that it'll ruin everybody and end the War."

"Do you know where they're printing it?" demanded Ole Devil.

"You might save your neck if you do," the girl went on.

"It's being printed down in New Orleans!" Ludlow blurted out.

"That's a mighty big area, but one well-covered by our spies," Belle pointed out. "How is it that they've learned nothing about the plot?"

"It's been kept a real close secret."

"Then how did you learn about it?" the girl snapped.

"Pickings've been mighty slim in New Orleans since the Yankees took it. So I grabbed when Gilpin came up with an offer to make some money. They didn't tell me much, but I learned what the game was and all about it."

"Go on," the girl prompted, knowing a man like Ludlow would have methods of gaining information that exceeded those of her own people; especially as he found himself with such a good starting point.

"Like I said," he continued, "I kept my eyes open and followed Gilpin without his knowing. I learned all the game, including where they're printing and holding the money."

"And where is it?" Belle asked.

"Is this important enough to save me?" inquired Ludlow.

"If you're telling the truth."

"I'm telling it, so help me!" Ludlow insisted, with such sincerity that the girl felt sure he told the truth. "A feller called Gaton's doing the printing and the stuff's held at his place on St. Charles Avenue."

"That's in the old city," Belle pointed out.

"Sure. A big old house standing in a garden with a high wall around it," agreed Ludlow. "Gaton's working for the Yankees, has been ever since they took over. That's the truth, Miss Boyd."

"I hope for your sake that it is," the girl said quietly.

"How about him, Miss Boyd?" Ole Devil asked.

"I'd say keep him alive, but a prisoner, until we've found a way to verify his story," the girl replied. "If it's true, turn him loose. If not—."

"If not you won't need to deal with him," Ole Devil growled. "I've men under me who learned torture from the Indians. We'll see if they can make him tell the truth. I'll do what you say. Release him, Dustine."

"Yo!" Dusty answered and obeyed.

After releasing Ludlow, Dusty left the cabin, fastening its door with the padlock which took the place of the usual fitting. Then he walked after the others in the direction of the house used as Ole Devil's headquarters.

"He talked easy enough," Dusty commented as he caught up to Belle.

"Easier than I expected," Tolling admitted.

"Of course he was only doing it for money," Belle put in. "That kind break easier than a fanatic. I'd have bet, when we watched him, that we wouldn't need to do more than threaten to use violence."

"Would you have carried out your threats, Belle?" Dusty inquired.

"If necessary," the girl replied quietly. "This isn't a game I play, Dusty, it's a vicious, dirty business without any rules. The thing now is to destroy the counterfeiting plant, its plates, inks and paper. If we can do that, it'll put back the Yankees' plot for long enough to allow us to counter it."

"Can your people handle it, Miss Boyd?" Ole Devil asked.

"I mean to try, General," she replied.

"You?"

"Of course. I know New Orleans fairly well, but I may need help."

"You want for me to go with you, Miss Boyd?" Tolling wanted to know.

"No. I'd like you to go into the Indian Nations and see if you can find out who Oliver was to contact. I don't think you're going to be any too happy about me, General Hardin."

"Why?" said the General.

"Because I'm going to make a formal request that you assign Dusty to help me wreck that plant."

"You realise what you're asking, Miss Boyd?" Ole Devil snapped, halting and facing the girl. "I know Dustine helped you collect those arms, but he travelled and worked in uniform. That won't be possible this time."

Which meant, as Dusty knew without needing telling, that if he fell into the Yankees' hands, he could not claim the rights and privileges accorded to a captured officer. If he went in civilian clothing, he classed as a spy and would be shot. For all that, Dusty felt a touch of pride when considering Belle Boyd, the fabled Rebel Spy, requested his assistance on a desperate and dangerous mission.

Ole Devil did not appear so eager. "Do you consider Dustine's presence necessary, Miss Boyd?"

"Essential, General," the girl assured him. "I need a man of courage and on whom I can rely implicitly. Dusty fills that need."

A frown creased Ole Devil's face. Apart from personal considerations, he had his command to consider. Losing Dusty for a further indefinite period would lessen his fighting strength and the balance of power hung delicately in Arkansas. However he realised that should the Yankee counterfeiting plant not be destroyed, the War must be lost. He also appreciated the risks and difficulties facing Belle. Having a good man—which, despite his youth, Dusty was—at her back might make the difference between success and failure. So he made his decision.

"Very well, Dustine," he said. "You will accompany Miss Boyd and give her every possible aid. Good luck to you both."

"Thank you, General," smiled the girl. "I've a feeling we'll likely need it."

CHAPTER SIX

A Different Way of Travelling

Due to the urgency of the situation neither Dusty nor Belle found time to sleep much on the night of Ludlow's interrogation. They had their preparations to make for the journey. First they would ride to the nearest town on the Red River and there go by steamboat down to Alexandria, after which some way must be found by which they could reach New Orleans.

During the first stages of the journey, Dusty would travel in uniform. To avoid attracting too much attention, he elected to wear a jacket which followed the dictates of the Confederate States Army's *Manual of Dress Regulations*, including the issue-type sword and pistol belt. His dress for New Orleans would be civilian clothing of a fairly nondescript kind; town suit, boots and hat. Nor could he take along his gunbelt and matched Army Colts as they would attract too much unwanted attention. That left him with the problem of selecting a suitable weapon for his needs. Texas born and raised, Dusty believed in a gun of .44 calibre as

61

the only type on which a man might place complete reliability. Yet none of them were small enough for easy concealment. Finally he elected to take along one Army Colt. It would be carried in his waistband, hidden under his jacket and be readily accessible when needed. Of course he would be unable to draw with his usual speed, but reckoned to be fast enough when dealing with men unused to range-style gun-handling.

Belle too make her preparations for the assignment. It seemed highly unlikely that she would need her specially designed ball gown, so she decided to leave it behind until her return. Instead she would travel to Alexandria in an outfit suited to the part she intended to play; that of a well-to-do Southern lady on a journey. In addition she meant to take her male clothing, gunbelt and another of her special dresses, this time of a cheaper appearance and cut on the style a lady's maid would wear. Using a capacious carpetbag as her one item of luggage, the girl packed in her spare clothing on top of the gunbelt and Dance. Already inside lay a jewellery case holding the "Borgia" ring, her lens locket and various trinkets. The parasol, taken down into its two parts went in the bag, as did a purse heavy with Yankee gold and a spare wig. She left the materials for destruction of the counterfeiting plant to be supplied by the South's agents in New Orleans.

So quickly did they work that on the night following the capture of Ludlow, Dusty and Belle boarded a riverboat and started upon the first and easiest leg of their journey.

While the boat carried him down the Red River, Dusty spent much of his waking time wondering what means they would use to reach New Orleans. In July the previous year, the Yankees finally took Vicksburg and gained control of the lower Mississippi River. On their last assignment Dusty and Belle avoided the problem that this posed by going along the Atchafalaya River to Morgan City, so by-passing the Big Muddy completely. Unfortunately they could hardly do so to reach New Orleans. Confederate armoured riverboats raided along the Mississippi, even slipping by the shore-batteries at Vicksburg and Baton Rouge to attack Yankee shipping on the lower reaches, but did not meet Dusty and Belle's needs. Running the gauntlet of the Yankee heavy artillery, or the U.S. Navy's efficient Mississippi Squadron would be too risky in a big river-boat when they had so much at stake. Of course they might take horses and pass along the fringe of the Yankee-held territory, then try to slip through to New Orleans over-land, but doing so was certain to take far too long to be of any use.

As the last major Confederate town on the Red before it joined the Mississippi, Alexandria lived in a constant state of readiness for war. On the down-stream side batteries of heavy-calibre cannon covered the water ready to repel any Yankee attack. Armoured vessels occupied most of the berths which before the War housed steamboats loaded with cotton and flatboats carrying produce of lesser importance down to the major cities along the country's greatest waterway.

On her arrival, Belle presented her credentials to the relevant authorities. She left Dusty to be taken on a tour of the city's defences while she saw various officials to arrange for their passage to New Orleans. Knowing something of Alexandria's defences, the girl made a request and backed it with Ole Devil's written orders that she be given every assistance. The General's name packed enough weight to ensure compliance and he arranged for a different way of travelling to any that Dusty might have guessed.

Shortly after dark Belle and Dusty entered a closed carriage and drove through the town. The girl wore male clothing and Dusty dressed as a civilian. With a range-dweller's sense of direction, Dusty guessed that they did not head for the main riverfront area. In fact they left Alexandria behind and went down-river. At last the carriage halted and they climbed down. Before them a narrow path wound off through a thickly wooded area. Standing in the centre of the path, a tall, slim, bearded young Confederate Navy lieutenant armed with sword and Navy Colt faced them.

"This's Lieutenant Cord Pinckney, Dusty," introduced Belle. "Cord, allow me to present Captain Dusty Fog."

"Captain Fog," greeted Pinckney. "Excuse the lack of formalities, but we'd best be moving."

Without saying more, Pinckney led the way along the winding path. Water glinted through the trees, a large lagoon off the main flow of the Red. At the lagoon's edge rested a kind of vessel Dusty had heard about but never before seen.

"A submersible," he said. "So that's how we'll do it!"

"That's just how we're going to do it," agreed the girl. "This is the Confederate Navy Ship *Jack the Giant-Killer.* Lieutenant Pinckney designed her himself specially for river work."

Basically the *Jack* looked little different to the other *David*-class torpedo boat-rams which operated off Charleston and gave the blockading Yankees as much trouble as did Dusty's Company in Arkansas. Fifty-four foot in length, she looked like a cigar with an oblong cockpit, funnel and torpedo-elevating spar rising from her deck. The torpedo itself, a copper container holding 100 pounds of gunpowder, rode submerged at the end of a fourteen foot hollow iron tube fitted to the bows, but could be raised to an operative position when needed. However the *Jack* rode higher in the water than the usual *David* which was ballasted down so hardly more than the cockpit showed above the surface.

Although smaller than any steamboat, the *Jack* still would show up on the river surface. Or so Dusty imagined as he looked at the little vessel. He was given no time to think of the matter. Already the *Jack*'s three-man crew stood by ready to leave. Smoke rose from the stack and the stoker tossed fuel on to the furnace, but its mouth had been masked so that none of the glow showed outside the hull.

"It'll not be as comfortable as travelling in a riverboat," Pinckney commented as his coxswain took the passengers' bags and stowed them at the rear of the cockpit. "And I hadn't counted on one of you being a lady."

"Neither did my father when I was born," Belle smiled. "He learned to live with it. I'm used to travelling rough, Mr. Pinckney."

"It'll be that," Pinckney replied. "We'll travel all night and as far as we dare during the day. It'll be uncomfortable, dangerous and uncertain. I've my orders to deliver you to New Orleans and aim to make a try. But I feel it's my duty to warn you of the dangers involved."

"And we accept them," Belle assured him. "Where do you want us to ride?"

Not that there would be much of a choice, the *Jack*'s sole accomodation being the tiny cockpit.

"Sit at the stern, the back end," ordered Pinckney, translating for the benefit of folks he did not expect to understand nautical terms. "Once we're under way, you can move about—as much as possible—unless we sight the enemy."

"And if we do?" asked Dusty, wondering what the tiny vessel could hope to accomplish against even one of the small 'tin-clad' river gun-boats, so-called because of their very light armour plating.

"You'll return to the stern, sit down and keep quiet," Pinckney replied. "I hope it doesn't come to that, though."

With his passengers aboard, Pinckney ordered his men to cast off. Despite using a rear-screw, as opposed to the twin side-wheels of the riverboats, the *Jack* handled well and showed a surprising manoeuvrability. After being poled away from the shore, the little submersible gathered way and headed across the lagoon. Ahead lay a narrow gap barely wide enough for the boat, but Pinckney guided it through with little change of speed and once on the river headed downstream.

Clearly the *Jack*'s crew knew their work and went about it without needing orders. In addition to their cutlasses and Navy Colts, the men had two shotguns and a pair of Sharps carbines for armament.

"Which same stops us coming alongside and trading broadsides with any Yankee we meet," Pinckney drawled as he saw Dusty studying his ship's weapons. "Mind you though, apart from those Yankee steam-launches, there's not a craft on the Big Muddy can catch the *Jack* running with the current and we'd give a launch a good run for its money."

Even as Pinckney spoke, one of the crew men hauled on a cable which raised the torpedo spar from the water. Then the sailor swung over the cockpit and advanced along the deck to stand by the elevating spar. He looked down at the water intently, giving an occasional direction over his shoulder to the coxswain. On shore the shapes of the guardian batteries showed, gun crews on the alert but not challenging the little ship.

"We're passing through the frame-torpedoes," Belle breathed. "That's why they raised the spar."

Dusty did not need to ask why. Frame-torpedoes—the name "mine" had not yet come into use—were copper or cast-iron shells filled with explosives, mounted on wooden frames firmly anchored to the river's bottom. Fixed to come just below the surface, the shells carried percussion caps to be ignited when struck by an enemy vessel coming up-river. However it did not pay to knock or jolt the torpedoes from any angle and Pinckney took no chances.

Even the *Jack*'s crew members looked relieved when they had passed through the frame-torpedo maze. On went the little boat, its screw propeller making only a small sound instead of the thrashing thump a side-wheeler's paddles gave out. With the current behind them and the engine turning the propellors steadily, they made a steady fifteen miles an hour.

Suddenly Dusty heard a gurgling sound and became aware that the *Jack* appeared to be settling deeper in the water. None of the crew showed the slightest concern, although the cox'n turned the wheel over to Pinckney and watched the river's surface creeping higher. At last, with the water lapping at the very bottom of the cockpit, the gurgling stopped. Pinckney swung the wheel and the *Jack* moved across the river, turned back and resumed its course down-

stream. Nodding in satisfaction, Pinckney gave an order and
the smallest member of his crew ducked out of sight under
the deck. Turning over the wheel to his cox'n, Pinckney
smiled at his passengers. It seemed that he noticed their
agitation for the first time.

"I've just been ballasting her down," he explained. "Run
water into two tanks so that we lay lower and aren't so easy
to see. Most of the time we'll be at normal level, but we'll
have to go down when we're passing Yankee ships or batteries. When we're by, we pump out the water and go on
as before."

"That's smart thinking," Dusty drawled, trying not to
reveal that he had been worried.

"The *Hunley* was a better one," Pinckney answered.
"She'd got right under water. The crew stayed down for
just over two and a half hours once."

"If we could have found some way to power her, it would
have made all the difference," Belle remarked.

"It'll come one of these days," prophesised Pinckney.

Even in Arkansas word of the submarine *Hunley*'s ex-
ploits had been heard. Lacking engines, for steam could not
be generated under water, the crew operated handles on a
crank shaft to propel it through the water. After experi-
mentation and some loss of life, the *Hunley* went down in
a successful attempt to destroy the U.S.S. *Housatonic*.

While unable to submerge completely, the little *David*-
class boats achieved greater success than the true submarine.

Despite the fact that the Red River remained in Confederate hands, one member of the tiny crew stayed on the
look-out all the time. The U.S. Navy's Mississippi Squadron
sometimes sent raiding vessels off the main river and even
a steam-launch's crew submerged to cockpit level, crept by
the Confederate batteries guarding the mouth of the Red
and swung out on to the wide Mississippi.

"I never knew it was this big!" Dusty breathed as daylight
gave him his first view of the main river.

"It's even wider lower down," the girl replied, then looked

at Pinckney. "What do we do now?"

"Go on as far as we can, then find a place to lie up until night-fall," he replied. "We have to pass the towns at night, the Yankees have garrisons in some of them."

Dusty and Belle exchanged glances. All too well they realised the extreme urgency of their mission; and understood what such an extensive delay might cost the South. Yet there did not seem to be any way of slipping unseen by the Yankee garrisons along the river's banks.

While thinking about the problem, Dusty glanced upstream and saw something bobbing in the current some way behind them. Even as he opened his mouth to give a warning, he realised the thing was a large tree either cut or torn down up-river and, having fallen in, came floating down on the current. From the lack of interest in the sight shown by the *Jack*'s crew, Dusty concluded it must be a reasonably regular occurrence. Pinckney confirmed the view when Dusty put a question to him.

"Trees? Sure, you see plenty of them; bushes too. I've seen what looked like whole islands floating down-river at times."

"Reckon the Yankees'd be used to seeing them, then," Dusty drawled.

"I'd say so," agreed Pinckney.

Looking at the wooded banks of the river, Dusty sucked in a breath. He did not wish to appear foolish and hesitated before offering what might be an impractical suggestion.

"I've got a fool notion that you might like to try, Mr. Pinckney," he said, and after explaining it finished, "Mind, I don't know sic 'em about boats or if it'll be possible to do."

"It'd be possible all right, but riskier than all hell," Pinckney answered. "Just how important is this mission you're on, Miss Boyd?"

"So important that its failure could cost us the war," Belle told him. "And any delay increases the danger."

"Then it's important for us to take the chance," Pinckney

decided. "We'll give your 'fool notion' a whirl, Captain
Fog. Take her ashore, cox'n."

Deftly swinging the *Jack* nearer to the bank, the cox'n
watched for a place where there would be sufficient water
close in for them to stop without running aground. Not until
two miles fell behind them did he find the kind of place he
wanted and during that time Pinckney explained Dusty's
scheme to his attentive crew. If the grins of the three men
proved anything, they felt no concern at chancing their lives
to the small Texan's 'fool notion.'

With the *Jack* bobbing in a bay just deep enough to keep
her afloat, but offering some slight shelter should any Yankee warship happen to pass, the party went to work. Taking
the field glasses used by the look-out, Belle went to a place
from which she could keep watch on the river and left the
men to handle the work. Putting aside all thought of rank,
Dusty and Pinckney helped the three enlisted men to cut
branches and bushes, then take the material to the boat.
With a sense of urgency driving them, the men secured their
gatherings until all the upper deck and its fittings lay hidden
under a ragged, yet natural-appearing, mass of vegetation.
While the sailors added the finishing touches, Pinckney and
Dusty discussed the dangers which lay ahead.

"We'll have to go with the current when anybody's watching," the lieutenant warned. "And stay as far away as possible from whoever is watching. It'd be best if we ran by
Baton Rouge in the dark, too. The Yankees only have small
garrisons in most places, but they hold the major cities with
strong forces."

"How about fuel?" asked Dusty.

"We'll need to pick some up. I know of a couple of secret
supplies left by the cutting parties from the different woodings."

Having made a long trip on a riverboat, Dusty knew
about woodings. Professional wood-cutters made their living by hewing timber and collecting it at established points
along the river for sale to passing boats. Pinckney explained

that the Yankees destroyed some of the woodings, but maintained others to supply fuel for their vessels. Under the guise of co-operating, some of the wooding owners laid on secret wood-piles for use by such Confederate ships as might need it while on raiding missions along the river.

With everything ready, the party ate a meal made up from supplies brought aboard in Alexandria. Then they boarded the foliage-draped *Jack* and started moving once more. After a few adjustments had been made, the cox'n announced that he could see well enough and discovered that the boat answered to the wheel in a satisfactory manner.

For three hours they travelled downstream without seeing anything to disturb them. Before the War there would have been other boats on the move, people working on the banks, but most activity had been suspended due to the danger of becoming involved in a clash between the two opposing forces. Suddenly the look-out turned from where he peered through a gap made in the foliage.

"Boat dead ahead, sir," he said, offering Pinckney the field glasses.

"Stop engines!" the lieutenant ordered after studying the approaching vessel briefly. "Run us as close as you can to the starboard bank, cox'n. Not a sound or movement from any of you after that."

With the engine stopped, the *Jack* drifted on the current. Gradually and in as near a natural manner as he could manage, the cox'n steered them across the river and then held the boat so that it continued to move but did not swing in the direction of the approaching enemy craft.

"It's a steam-launch," breathed the sailor at Dusty's side as they peered through the foliage.

Dusty studied the other craft as it drew nearer, holding out in the centre of the wide river and making good speed even against the current. In appearance it resembled a large rowing boat, but with a powerful steam-engine installed. A twelve-pounder boat-howitzer rode on a slide-carriage at the bows, while the launch's spar torpedo hung on slings alongside instead of extending before the vessel as it would when ready for use. Although only thirty foot in length, the steam-launch carried a crew of seven men and possessed sufficient armament to blow the *Jack* out of the water even without using the spar-torpedo.

Nothing Dusty had ever done in action or during his patrols ever filled him with a nervous strain to equal that of watching the Yankee steam-launch go by. Born on the great open plains of Southern Texas, the largest river he had seen until joining the Army was the Rio Hondo and that looked like no more than a stream compared with the width of the Big Muddy. His eyes flickered to the Sharps carbines and his right hand touched the grip of the Army Colt at his waistband. Neither weapon offered much comfort when he considered the strength of the enemy's armament.

Belle could sense Dusty's tension and smiled a little, which helped relieve her own. However, having seen the small Texan's cold courage at other times, she knew he would do nothing that might endanger their mission.

On came the launch, drawing closer, coming level and then passing them. Not one of the Yankee sailors did more than glance at the floating foliage. Soon the two vessels lay so far apart that Pinckney decided they might chance using their own engines. With the added thrust of the *Jack*'s pro-pellors, they quickly ran the Yankee launch out of sight.

"How'd you like it, Captain Fog?" grinned Pinckney.

"Well, I'll tell you," drawled Dusty sincerely. "Give me leading a cavalry charge any old time at all."

CHAPTER SEVEN

A Matter of Simple Priorities

The *Jack* continued to make good time, without meeting any other shipping or needing to do more than cut off their engines while passing some river-edge town or village. At around three in the afternoon, Pinckney told his passengers that they would soon be stopping to take on fuel at a secret dump left by Confederate supporters working out of Mendel's wooding.

"We'll have to run in there behind that island," he went on, pointing ahead. "Unless it's silted up or something, there's more than enough room and water for the *Jack* and we'll be hidden from anybody who might happen to be coming along the river in either direction."

"It may be as well to take a look before we pull in," Dusty suggested. "If you put me ashore, I'll go."

"Two pairs of eyes are better than one," Belle remarked. "I'll go with you."

"Follow the bank then," Pinckney told them. "You'll see a flowering dogwood tree about a hundred yards along it and the wood-pile's hidden under a dead-fall near to it."

"Mind if I take one of the carbines?" Dusty asked. "A dead-fall's a good place to find a bear, if you have bear down here."

"We've some," admitted Pinckney. "But there's a Yankee garrison at Mendel's Wooding and if they hear a shot, they'll come running."

"Looks like a carbine won't help us then, Dusty," Belle said and opened her bag to take out the parasol handle. "It doesn't make any noise—."

"And won't stop a bear, either," grinned Dusty. "We'll just have to hope there's not one there."

"I'll come with you," Pinckney decided. "I know just where the wood is and can tell whether it'll be any use to us."

Parting the foliage, Dusty, Belle and Pinckney slipped through, into the water and waded ashore. Back on his native element, Dusty moved with easy confidence, gliding ahead of the other two and searching around him with careful, all-seeing eyes. Coming to a halt, he waited for the other two and pointed ahead.

"'Gator," he said. "Just look at the size of it, too."

Belle and Pinckney were more used to seeing alligators, but admitted to themselves that the specimen ahead could be termed a real big one. Full sixteen feet long, with a bulk which told of good feeding and long years, the alligator lay with its broad, rounded and flat-looking snout pointing to the water of the channel. Hearing Dusty's voice, it lifted its powerful body on legs which appeared too slender to support it. Letting out a long hiss, it plunged into the channel's water to create a considerable disturbance before disappearing under the surface.

As the water parted under the impact of the alligator's arrival, something black, rounded and inanimate showed briefly above the surface. Briefly or not, Belle and Pinckney saw enough.

"A torpedo of some kind!" the girl exclaimed.

"Looks that way," agreed Pinckney.

"Then the Yankees have found the wood-pile," Dusty growled.

"Not necessarily," Pinckney replied. "They'd figure this channel'd be a place where one of our raiders might hide and left a torpedo here instead of having to guard it."

"We'll have to move it before we can fetch the *Jack* in," Belle stated.

"That's just what we'll have to do," agreed Pinckney quietly.

"Can you do it?" the girl asked.

"I've had to do it a couple of times."

"It might be as well for us to make sure there's enough wood on hand for it to be worth while," Dusty commented.

"There's that," Pinckney agreed.

Going first to the flowering dogwood tree and then making a circle of the dead-fall, Dusty found no sign of new or old tracks which would tell that the hidden wood had been discovered. While he did not put himself in Kiowa's class as a reader of signs, Dusty reckoned he knew enough to locate any left by inexperienced men. Finding nothing, he went to the dead-fall—a tree fetched down in a storm and supported on a clump of rock in such a manner that a hollow remained underneath. Under the dead-fall, hidden by what looked like part of the tree's branches, lay piles of cut timber. Calling up the others, Dusty told them of his negative findings. Then he stepped aside and allowed Pinckney to take his place.

"What'd you expect to find?" Dusty asked, after the lieutenant rose from examining the wood.

"An old riverboat trick was to hollow out a log, fill it with gunpowder then plug up the end so it looked natural," Pinckney explained. "Then when the stokers tossed it on to the boiler fire—."

"I don't reckon it did the boilers any good," grinned

Dusty. "Is this lot all right?"

"As far as I can see," Pinckney replied. "Let's see about that torpedo."

"What kind is it?" asked Belle.

"I didn't see much," Pinckney answered. "But I reckon it's a Brooke, or a copy of it. The Yankees've fetched a few in unexploded, I'd say."

"They might know about Turtle torpedoes too," warned the girl.

"Hell's fire, yes," Pinckney barked. "I'd forgotten all about them."

"What're they?" Dusty asked.

Belle explained how the Brooke torpedo consisted of a copper case holding the explosive charge and bearing either percussion or chemical detonators positioned to be struck when a passing boat made contact. As an added aid to the built-in buoyancy chamber, the Brooke rode on a wooden-spar that extended down to its anchor; which made the fast-developing art of mine-sweeping more difficult. As an added precaution against removal, the Turtle torpedo had been developed. Looking roughly like a turtle's shell, the torpedo lay on the bottom with a length of wire connecting its detonating primer to the Brooke. Should anyone attempt to drag away the Brooke torpedo, its weight activated the Turtle's primer and one hundred pounds of explosive went off beneath the surface.

"So we'll have to send a man down to check," the girl concluded. "And if there is a Turtle, he'll have to cut it free."

"Which's dangerous," Pinckney continued. "The Brooke might've moved and pulled on the Turtle's primer so that a touch sends it off. If that happens while I'm cutting the wire—."

"In that case," Dusty interrupted. "You'd best let me do it."

"You?" asked Pinckney.

"It's a matter of simple priorities," Dusty replied. "You

can't be spared, Cord, or there'll be nobody to run your
boat. Nor can any of your crew. And Belle has to reach
New Orleans. I can't handle her work. So that makes me
the most expendable of us."

True enough, as a matter of pure, cold-blooded logic,
but not the kind of decision most men would have cared to
make.

"How well can you swim, Dusty?" Pinckney asked, dropping the formal mode of address for the first time.

"Well enough, under and on top of the water. Tell me
what to look for and how to handle it, then I'll have a try."

"I've got some wire cutters in the *Jack*—."

"Let me fetch them," Belle suggested.. "You tell Dusty
what to do."

"Go to it," Pinckney confirmed and after the girl left
went on, "find the Brooke, but don't touch it. Then if you
dive you can follow its spar to the anchor. I don't reckon
the water'll be more than ten, twelve foot deep if that. Feel
real carefully around the anchor until you touch the Turtle's
connecting wire. Then come up and let me know what you
find."

Stripping off all but his underpants, Dusty entered the
water. Pinckney watched and decided that the small Texan
could swim well enough to handle the work ahead. On
locating the Brooke, which—being designed to handle shal-
low-draught riverboats—did not lie too deep, Dusty sucked
in a breath and dived. He found little difficulty in locating
the anchor, merely following the wooden spar down to the
bed of the channel. Before his air ran out, he traced the
edge of the anchor block and felt the thin wire. With cold
apprehension he realised that the connection between the
anchor and the torpedo was taut.

Long practice had taught Dusty to keep his eyes open
under water and he could see a little way in the dark canal.
Forcing himself to stay down, he kept one finger touching
the wire as he followed it from the Brooke. Not three feet
away lay the rounded shape of the Turtle. Before Dusty

could do anything more, lack of air sent him to the surface. By that time Belle had returned, but she swung her back to Dusty as he broke water and gasped in a long breath.

"It's a torpedo," Dusty declared. "With a Turtle on the bottom. The wire's taut, too."

"That's bad!" Picnkney growled.

"Maybe," Dusty said. "I'm going to try to lift the Turtle and move it closer to the Brooke, then cut the wire."

"That'll be risky!" Belle gasped, throwing aside the proprieties and turning to face Dusty.

"No more risky than cutting the wire while it's tight," Dusty pointed out and dived again.

Going down seemed longer, but Dusty forced himself to concentrate on his object. He found the Turtle and lowered his hands, fingers probing around its edges and finding them partly buried in the gravel bottom of the channel. At last he managed to get a grip on the underneath. By that time his lungs felt on the point of bursting, but he forced himself to carry on. Going up for air and diving again would not be easy and he preferred to get the business over in one go if he possibly could. So he tightened his grip and lifted. For an instant the Turtle remained stuck, but then it moved. Dusty forced himself to think, not acting blindly. Whatever he did, he must move the Turtle towards the Brooke. If he drew it away, the pressure might pull hard enough to operate the primer and fire the charge.

Slowly the Turtle rose and moved in the direction of the Brooke's anchor. Setting down his burden, Dusty gently felt for the wire. Relief flooded through him as he found it to be hanging loose. The main danger had passed. All that remained to do was clip the wire and remove the Brooke torpedo. Gratefully Dusty rose once more to the surface. One look at his face told the watching pair of his success without needing words.

"Pass me the wire clippers, Belle," Dusty requested. "I reckon it's safe to cut them apart now."

"Everything's all right then?" she asked, handing him

the powerful instruments collected from the *Jack*.

"I'll tell you better the next time I come up," Dusty grinned. "If I come up slow enough that is."

"You be careful!" Belle ordered. "If anything happens to you, it's me who will have to go back and explain to Company 'C.'"

"Now there's concern for you, Dusty," Pinckney chuckled.

Once again Dusty dived down through the water, following the Brooke's spar until he could see the Turtle resting in its new position. However the task proved more difficult than he imagined. After three attempts Dusty managed to clamp the jaws of the clippers around the wire. Fighting against the time when lack of air would drive him back to the surface, he applied pressure on the handles. It must be a straight cut. Any jiggling or twisting at the wire in an attempt to weaken it might drag out the primer and explode the Turtle. Then the wire parted, its separated ends falling away.

Even as Dusty realised he had completed his task, a feeling that all was not well bit into him. As his danger-instinct screamed out its grim warning, he became aware of a shape moving through the water in his direction and traveling with an ease that no human being ever attained under such conditions.

Since reaching a greater length than most others of its kind, the bull alligator ruled that stretch of the Mississippi and claimed the channel as its especial den area. While it might dive into the water at the approach of man, the alligator feared nothing when in its native element. Sensing the presence of another large creature under the channel's surface, it came back to defend its territory. Gliding forward with the effortless-seeming way of its kind, the alligator located Dusty and moved in to attack. With a thrust of its powerful tail, it surged in the small Texan's direction.

Never had Dusty's lightning-fast reactions stood up to such a test. From seeing the alligator rushing at him to doing something about it took only a split second. Nor would there have been time for any greater deliberation on the problem. Digging his feet into the channel's bed, Dusty propelled himself backwards. Yet so close was his escape that the alligator brushed against him in passing. Desperately Dusty threw one arm around the alligator's thick neck, while his legs locked around the rough scaled body. With his grip established, Dusty hung safe from the brute's jaws and tail; but felt like the man who caught a tiger by the tail. If he released his hold, the alligator would turn on him again.

"I think he's going to make it!" breathed Belle as the seconds ticked by.

Suddenly the even surface of the water bulged and churned. Once more the Brooke torpedo's head showed briefly, but neither Belle nor Pinckney had eyes for it. Both stared at the sight of Dusty clinging to the alligator as they swirled into sight and disappeared once more beneath the surface.

"Lord!" Belle gasped, reaching for her Dance. "We forgot that bull 'gator!"

Although both she and Pinckney drew their weapons, neither offered to fire. Not only could they see no sign of Dusty, but both realised that the sound of shooting would attract any nearby Yankees as effectively as if the torpedoes went off. If it came to a point, Belle doubted her ability to hit the alligator in its brief appearances, with Dusty clinging so close to it.

"Bring me a cutlass, cox'n!" Pinckney yelled, reaching the same conclusion as Belle and aware that the weapon's arrival might come too late.

Equally aware, Belle made her decision. Swiftly she twirled the Dance back into its holster, then unbuckled and allowed the belt to slide to her feet. Darting forward, she gripped the metal ball of the parasol handle, tugging to draw out the full wicked length of the billy. Even as Pinckney realised what the girl meant to do and opened his mouth to order her back, Belle plunged into the water.

Rising again Dusty and the alligator rolled into sight, the small Texan being raised clear of the surface. Although Belle struck out hard, she knew she would reach the spot too late for that appearance. Then something happened which lent an added urgency to the need for rescuing Dusty. Lashing around, the alligator's tail struck the water scant inches from the Brooke torpedo's head. If the tail struck, or the brute's body collided with the swaying torpedo, an explosion must surely result. Once more man and reptile disappeared beneath the boiling surface of the channel. Belle swam closer, conscious of her own danger. While Dusty held the neck and body, he could not grip and keep closed the murderous jaws. Seeing the girl's arms or legs as she swam, it might grab hold of her.

The danger did not take form and Belle saw the struggling pair rising to the surface. Treading water, she watched and waited. Up they rolled, with the small Texan retaining his hold with grim and deadly determination. Stripped to his underpants, his powerful muscular development showed. Biceps bulged, their veins standing out from the skin, under the effort of holding on. Dusty's face showed strain and approaching exhaustion as he opened his mouth to drag air into his tortured lungs. Yet he still retained his hold and did not seem aware of Belle's nearness.

Sucking in her breath, the girl took aim and struck with all her might. The force of her effort caused her body to rise in the water. Around, up and down lashed the murderous billy. Its coil-spring bowed and snapped straight, propelling the pliant but powerful steel shaft with increasing force. All too well Belle knew the danger. If the metal ball of the billy caught Dusty's arm, it would splinter bone and cause him to lose his hold.

Never had the billy seemed to move so slowly. Then it descended, the ball smashing on to the top and centre of the alligator's skull. Although unaware of the girl's arrival, Dusty heard the wicked crack of impact and felt a convulsive shudder run through the alligator's giant frame.

"Let go, Dusty!" Belle screeched. "Turn him loose and head for the bank."

The words meant nothing to Dusty in his dazed, half-drowned condition. Yet he sensed a difference in the alligator's behaviour as it began to sink again. Instead of forging its way down, the reptile sank slowly and in a limp manner.

Flinging her billy ashore, Belle dived after and caught Dusty under the armpits in an effort to drag him back to the surface. She failed to do so, but help came fast. Disregarding the cutlass his cox'n waved while dashing along the bank, Pinckney also discarded his belt—he had removed his sword on entering the *Jack* so as to conserve the boat's limited space—and plunged into the water. Striking out fast, Pinckney reached Belle and dived under to help. Between them, Belle and Pinckney managed to haul Dusty back to the surface. In his half-drowned condition, the small Texan could not maintain his hold on the alligator. As he felt the body slip away from him, Dusty's head broke the surface and he sucked in air. On being released, the alligator's body continued to sink until it came to rest on the bed of the channel.

Belle and Pinckney hauled Dusty towards the bank, while the cox'n plunged forward, wading in to lend them a hand. A few seconds later Dusty lay on solid land and looked weakly up at the anxious faces around him.

"Wh—Where's the 'gator?" he gasped

"Belle got it," Pinckney replied. "Although I'm damned if I know how she did it."

"I just whomped that ole 'gator over the head with my billy," the girl smiled. "It's not the first time I've done it. When I was around eleven back on the plantation I and a boy cousin made a regular game of killing 'gators by sneaking up and cracking them over the skull with a piece of timber. Lordy me! I'll never forget mama's face when she learned how Willy and I carried on while we were out walking."

"Thanks, Belle," Dusty said. "And you, Cord. Lord, I'll

be old afore my time working with you pair."

For the first time Belle realised the exact scanty nature of Dusty's attire and came hurriedly to her feet. Nor did her soaking shirt and pants lead to modesty, so she decided to make adjustments and save embarrassment all round.

"I think I'd better find something dry to wear and go get changed into it," she said casually.

"Go to it," Pinckney replied. "We'll see to moving the Brooke, bring the *Jack* in and take on the fuel. You take a rest, Dusty, you've earned it."

Shortly before sundown the *Jack*, loaded with fuel and under the mass of foliage, crept out of the channel. Before leaving, Pinckney stripped the detonators from the torpedo and replaced its harmless shell back in position. If the Yankees had left the Brooke, they would find it in place should they check. Expecting the torpedo to be connected to the Turtle, it hardly seemed likely any inspecting crew would attempt to raise the Brooke in order to make a close examination. So they might continue to assume all was well and never suspect the guardian of the channel rode impotent and useless on its spar.

"Not that I'm ungrateful," Dusty drawled as the journey resumed. "But you could've got killed coming in to help me. The idea was for me to take all the risks and chance getting blown up."

"Like I said," Belle replied. "It would be me who had to face Company 'C' if anything happened to you."

"You think you've got problems," grinned Pinckney. "I'd not only've had Dusty's company after me, I'd be running from your bosses too, Belle, if that 'gator managed to kill both of you."

"Damned if I guessed it," Dusty said in a resigned voice. "But I had the least to worry about of us all."

CHAPTER EIGHT

A Snag to Miss Boyd's Plans

Before the War came, New Orleans ranked as the United States' second greatest port; and at the height of the cotton-gathering season its volume of trade exceeded even New York's. The city's waterfront area spread along the river for four miles and at times ocean-going or river-boats filled almost every inch of the frontage, in some cases lining out three or four deep. Then there had been a constant coming and going, boats arriving or departing with cargoes and helping the New Orleans banks to hold a greater combined capital than those of any city in the land, with the possible exception of gold-rich San Francisco.

The War changed all of that. When Farragut brought his fleet of iron-clad ships into the Mississippi, all hope of peaceful trading ended. Such riverboats as could fled up the river, others were sunk by the Yankee ironclads' guns. When defeat became inevitable, the waterfront glowed red as stocks of cotton, sugar, molasses and other produce were set on fire to prevent them falling into enemy hands.

Altogether the Federal garrison at New Orleans topped the fifteen thousand mark, the Mississippi Squadron numbered forty-three major vessels and many smaller craft. However their ships took up only a portion of the riverfront and much more lay empty, deserted, with blackened, gutted ruins bleakly facing the mighty river.

Shortly before midnight, three days after leaving Alexandria, the *Jack* crept through the darkness towards a derelict stretch of wharf. Ballasted down to the limit of safety, the little boat had wended its way past Yankee artillery batteries and by U.S. Navy guard ships. The covering of foliage which served them so well during the majority of the journey had been discarded that day at sundown and within sight of the city, for it would attract too much attention and might be investigated.

After disarming the Brooke torpedo and tangling with the alligator, the remainder of the trip proved uneventful. Once they lay up for two hours against a mud bank while a Yankee transport took on fuel at a wooding. During the second night they drifted silently by one of the big *Conestoga*-class gunboats, with Pinckney breathing curses at the turn of fate which made him pass up such a tempting and open target. The Yankee vessel went on its way, crewmen acting like they rode on a pleasure-cruise and blissfully unaware of the danger so narrowly averted.

As they approached the dock, a gurgling sound told Dusty that the *Jack* pumped out its ballast. Slowly the boat rose higher in the water, but instead of stopping edged between the piles of the wharf. An air of alert tension filled the *Jack*'s crew and the cox'n went forward with a hooded bull's-eye lantern in his hand. Standing on the wet deck forward, he darted an occasional glimmer of light by which Pinckney at the wheel steered. It was an eerie sensation, passing between the piles supporting the wharf. Then the light showed a small jetty and Pinckney brought his boat to a halt alongside it.

"This's as far as we go," he told his passengers in a low

voice. "Look around, cox'n and make sure all's secure."

"Aye aye, sir," the cox'n replied and stepped on to the jetty to fade away into the blackness.

"This's some place you have here, Cord," Dusty remarked when the cox'n returned with the news that all was safe.

"A bunch of us *David*-class captains rigged it up when we saw that New Orleans must fall," Pinckney replied. "We only use it in emergencies, but the Yankees haven't found it."

"How long can you lay here, Cord?" Belle asked.

"We're short on food, but I can stay until tomorrow night. Likely have to, there won't be time to run clear of the defences before morning. Will that be any good to you?"

"Hardly. It'll take all tomorrow at least to get what I need. If I can get food for you, are you game to wait two more nights?"

"I can get my own food," Pinckney assured her. "All right, I'll stay on for three days, but I'll have to pull out by just after sundown on the third night."

"Thank you, Cord," Belle said sincerely. "If we aren't back by then, go. In that case Dusty and I will take our chance of slipping through the Yankee lines and make our way north through our own territory."

"When do we start, Belle?" asked Dusty.

"Not before morning," the girl answered. "I don't know if the Yankees still impose a curfew, but even if they don't we'd attract attention walking through the streets at this hour."

"You sure would," agreed Pinckney. "I say grab some sleep and leave here at around eight or so in the morning. That way there'll be enough folks on the streets for you to have a chance."

"That's what we'll do," confirmed Belle. "And the sleep will be welcome."

Although the hidden dock offered none of the comforts of home, the *Jack*'s party slept well. Next morning Belle went behind some of the pilings and changed into one of her dresses. She then worked on a wig, altering its hairstyle to fit the part she must play. When finished, the girl looked like a lady's maid in the employment of a rich family. With her other property packed in the bag, she and Dusty accompanied the cox'n through a trapdoor cut in the floor of a gutted warehouse and came out on a deserted sidealley.

"Go down that ways and you'll come out on Thrift Street," the cox'n said. "Do you know it, ma'am?"

"Well enough to go to where I'm going," Belle answered.

"Good luck then," the man said, admiration on his face.

Dusty had often marvelled at the manner in which Belle could slough off her natural air of charm and good-breeding. On changing clothes she walked and talked like the wearer of such dress would.

Any doubts Belle might have felt about Dusty faded away. Without his uniform he became small, insignificant in appearance, an attribute he would turn to his advantage on more than one occasion during later years.*

"Where're we going?" he asked as they mingled with the early morning crowd on Thrift Street.

"To see one of our best agents," the girl replied, then raised her voice as a pair of Yankee soldiers approached them. "Don't you-all drop the bag, Jeremiah, or the mistress'll tan your fool hide for sure."

Neither of the soldiers, members of an infantry regiment on garrison duty in the city, as much as glanced at the passing pair. Dusty grinned at Belle and started to look back at the soldiers.

"Whooee!" he began. "I never thought to pass—."

"Don't look back!" Belle hissed. "Act like you're used to seeing Yankees around."

"Why sure," Dusty said. "I'm sorry, Belle."

One occasion is told in "The Floating Outfit."

"Don't be," the girl told him. "I'd make mistakes handling your work."

"Talking of that," Dusty drawled. "Do something nice for both of us in future, Belle gal."

"What?"

"Don't ask for me on another chore like this. It's plumb rough on the nerves."

A faint smile flickered across Belle's face at the words. Most spies felt concern when they passed through enemy-controlled streets. Certainly Dusty handled himself well, considering that it was his first mission.

Although the girl had to pause and think a couple of times and once ask a passing man for directions, she and Dusty made good time through the streets. They passed other Yankee soldiers and sailors, with Dusty studiously ignoring his enemies. To help take his mind off the tricky nature of their business, Belle told him something of the person they went to contact.

"Her name is Madam Lucienne and she runs what used to be one of the most popular—and expensive—dress shops in New Orleans."

"A dress shop?" Dusty asked, for the nature of the business did not seem to go with the dangerous work of spying.

"Don't sell her short," Belle smiled. "Madam Lucienne had a 'past,' or so Mama always used to tell me. Of course she never told me what the 'past' was; but you know what it means."

"It sure covers plenty of ground," Dusty replied.

Having a "past" might mean no more than coming from the wrong section of society, or gaining a divorce after an unfortunate marriage. Being connected with the theatre might also give a woman a "past," or any of a number of other things. Whatever aspect put Madam Lucienne in the category of having a "past," she appeared to have overcome it if she ran a successful business in the old city of New Orleans.

"'Past' or not," Belle said. "She's the best agent in New Orleans, with contacts all over the city."

"Reckon she can help us?"

"She probably knows about the counterfeiting plot already, if not of the plant's location. Even if she doesn't, she'll know where we can find the men we need for the work."

"I'd been wondering how you planned to handle things," Dusty remarked. "It looked like a chore for more than the two of us."

"It'll need more than us, for sure," Belle agreed. "We'll need somebody who knows how to break open the safe, for a starter."

"And Madam Lucienne knows somebody like that?"

"Knows the right man, or how to find him. We're nearly there, Dusty. It's around this corner and along the street."

Naturally the rich Creoles did not wish anything so sordid as a business section close to their homes; nor would they want to wander too far when shopping. The street on to which Belle and Dusty turned catered to the whims of the elegant and wealthy citizens. Before the War every shop along it would have been open and doing good business. Only a few remained in operation, but all seemed to find trade, if from a different class of customer.

Across the street from the shop bearing the discreet sign announcing that Madam Lucienne owned it, a smart carriage drawn by two good horses stood at the sidewalk. A colonel, wearing a uniform that carried the scarlet facings and trouser stripe of the artillery, escorted his wife into a milliner's shop, having just left the carriage. Apart from the colonel and his driver, a smartly-dressed artillery private, who already mounted the carriage seat again, there was no sign of Yankee troops. As the woman was in her late middle age, plump, homely and well-dressed, Dusty assumed her to be the officer's wife. The small Texan could also see how some of the street's occupants still found business.

It was Dusty's first visit to a big city shop and he found a big difference from the places to which he had become accustomed. Even in Arkansas, a comparatively civilized area, shops tended to be on the general store lines, with their wares exposed attractively on display. Not so in Madam Lucienne's exclusive establishment. Dusty could see no sign of the clothing she sold, only comfortable tables, chairs dotted about the tastefully-decorated front room, and fitting cubicles erected along the walls.

Behind the small, elegant counter which faced the front entrance stood a tall young man who failed to blend into the surroundings and looked out of place in the room. He wore a good suit, had a sallow, lean face with an expression of supercilious condescension, with lank long hair and a general impression of needing a good wash. Looking up from the thick, leather-bound ledger he was reading, the man studied Dusty and Belle.

"Is Madam Lucienne here, sir?" Belle asked mildly, ducking a curtsy to the man and her very attitude warned Dusty that all was not well.

"No," the young man answered, his voice holding a Northern accent. "I'm her—assistant."

Dusty darted a glance at Belle, finding her to be expressionless yet tense. While completely inexperienced in such matters, Dusty felt Madam Lucienne would be highly unlikely to accept such a man as her assistant in a fashionable business.

"I came to collect Mrs. Beauclaire's new ball gown," Belle told the man. "Is it ready yet?"

"Not right now."

Even as the man replied, a voice sounded from the open door behind him and which led into the rear of the building.

"It's no use, Kaddam. There's no sign of the old bitch's rec—!" While speaking, another tall, lean young man appeared at the door. Apart from a drooping moustache, he looked much like the first. Halting, he chopped off his words and looked across the counter. "Who're they?"

"Couple of servants," Kaddam replied. "Come after Mrs. Beauclaire's new ball gown."

"Get them out of here."

"You heard Mr. Turnpike. Get out."

"Yes, sir," Belle answered meekly, nudging Dusty in warning. "We'd best go, Jeremiah."

"Hold hard!" Turnpike barked as Belle started to turn.

"What's wrong, Melvin?" Kaddam asked.

"There's something about this I don't like," Turnpike answered and began to move forward, reaching into his jacket's right side pocket.

Moving with his usual speed, Dusty scooped up the heavy ledger—which Kaddam closed and laid aside on their entrance—and spun it sideways. Its hard edge caught Turnpike in the face, halting his advance and causing his right hand to emerge empty from the pocket.

In a continuation of the move Dusty's left hand slapped down on the counter top and he vaulted upwards. Kaddam began to take action a good five seconds too late. Out lashed Dusty's left leg, driving his boot full into Kaddam's advancing body. Caught in the chest by a solid boot heel, powered by a leg toughened from long hours of hard travelling, Kaddam croaked and reeled backwards. Going over the counter even as he kicked Kaddam, Dusty landed before Turnpike. Spluttering curses and spitting blood from his damaged lips, Turnpike threw a wild punch in Dusty's direction. Dusty ducked under the blow, slamming his right fist hard into Turnpike's solar plexus. With an agonised croak Turnpike went back and doubled over. On the heels of his first blow, Dusty whipped up his left hand to meet the down-swinging jaw. A click like two colossal billiard balls connecting sounded and Turnpike snapped erect once more. Glassy-eyed and limp, he shot back through the door and landed sprawled out on the floor.

Although Belle wished to avoid trouble, she realised that she must take a hand in Dusty's play. Leaping forward, she stamped her right foot on to the back of Kaddam's rear knee. Thrown off balance as his leg doubled under him, Kaddam went to his knees. Before the man could recover, Belle hitched up her skirt and kicked again. She sent her left foot crashing into the centre of Kaddam's shoulders and propelled him head first into the wall. When Kaddam hit the wall, he arrived with enough force to knock himself unconscious.

"Who are they?" Dusty asked as Kaddam collapsed limply to the floor.

"Some of Pinkerton's men," the girl answered. "They must have caught Madam."

"Looks that way. Or killed her. Reckon we ought to look around and see?"

"There's no time. They were looking for her records and more of them might be coming. She's not a prisoner here and we can't help her if she's dead. Empty the cash drawer, take the money with you."

"Make it look like we robbed the place, huh?" Dusty said.

"That's it," Belle agreed. "I'll take the ledger, what they were looking for is in it."

"Won't they think things when they find it's gone?" asked Dusty.

"We'll have to chance it and hope they think we took it along for the leather binding," Belle replied. "This's going to make things difficult for us, Dusty."

"It sure is," Dusty answered, scooping the money from the cash drawer into his jacket pocket. "What'll we do now?"

"Find someplace safe where we can look through this ledger and see what we can learn."

"And if we don't learn anything?"

"I'm trying not to think of *that*," Belle admitted frankly. "But if we don't I've another contact. He'd help for money, not through loyalty to the South."

Despite her calm words, Belle knew just how much harder

grew the situation. Yet, no matter what happened to her, Madam Lucienne would try to leave some message behind. On their previous meeting Lucienne had said if anything went wrong the ledger would tell Belle where to find help, but did not have a chance to explain how.

Picking up the book, Belle opened it and glanced at the first page. It held nothing but a list of customers' names, addresses and prices paid. Nor did the subsequent pages prove any more enlightening to the girl's rapid examination. Not that she really expected they would. Madam Lucienne would hardly make the prying loose of her secrets all that easy.

"I reckon we'd best get moving, Belle," Dusty said quietly.

"You're right," she replied, and tucked the book under her arm.

With Dusty carrying the girl's bag, they made for the door. Unnoticed behind them, Turnpike dragged himself to his feet. Almost maniacal rage mingled with the pain that twisted his face as he lurched to and leaned against the side of the door. From his pocket he drew one of the metal-cartridge firing .32 calibre Smith & Wesson revolvers popular among Northern supporters who hailed from the less firearm-conscious East, lined it at Dusty's back and fired a shot. Still feeling the effects of Dusty's handling, Turnpike did not have a steady hand. So his bullet passed between the pair without touching either of them, flying on to pass through a glass panel of the door.

At the sound of the shot, Dusty let Belle's bag drop and whirled around. His right hand fanned across, gripped the Colt's butt and slid the weapon from his waistband. Going into what would one day be known as the gun-fighter's crouch—Colt held waist high, in the centre of his body and aimed by instinctive alignment—he cut loose in the only manner possible under the circumstances: for a kill. Only one thing stood between Turnpike and death, the fact that Dusty carried his gun in a different manner than usual.

Drawing from the waistband made just the slight alteration which turned what should have been a bullet between the eyes to a nasty graze across the side of the head. Even so, Turnpike jerked back, spun around, and fell out of sight through the door.

"Get the hell out of here, Belle!" Dusty barked, unsure of how seriously he hit Turnpike and conscious that the other did not drop his gun before disappearing.

Swiftly Belle scooped up her bag, knowing Dusty might need both hands free, and darted to the door. Keeping his Colt lined on the opening behind the counter, Dusty followed. Without looking back, Belle jerked open the door and stepped out. Clearly the bullet breaking the window attracted attention. Across the street, the carriage's driver stood up on his seat and looked in the girl's direction. Not that he worried Belle; her interest centred on another pair of soldiers further down the street. Although cavalrymen, they were on foot and worked for the Provost Marshal's Department (Military Police as such did not yet exist). Their main function was dealing with breaches of the peace and acting in place of the normal New Orleans police.

On hearing the window break, the two men halted and waited to see what caused it. When Belle appeared, they started towards her. At that moment Dusty joined the girl. Although he no longer held his revolver, the soldiers increased their pace and slipped free their clubs. Dusty realised that to start shooting would not be advisable and glanced across the street.

"Head for the carriage, Belle!" he ordered.

Even though the driver saw Belle and Dusty headed his way, he took no action. Driving his commanding officer's carriage did not call for carrying weapons, so he wore neither sword nor revolver. Instead of making some move, he just stood up in the carriage and stared. Against a man like Dusty Fog such hesitation could only bring disaster. Bounding up on to the seat, Dusty lowered his head and butted the driver in the body. Taken by surprise, winded by the force of Dusty's attack, the driver shot backwards off the seat and landed rump-first on the sidewalk.

Belle pitched her bag into the back of the carriage and followed it. Before she could do more than enter, Dusty grabbed the reins and slapped them against the rumps of the two horses. There was not even time for him to feel grateful to a fate which put a sedentary non-combatant soldier as driver instead of a veteran who would have been far more difficult to handle.

"Yee-ah!" Dusty whooped. "Giddap there!"

A spirited pair, the horses needed no further encouragement. Lunging forward, they threw their weight into the harness and almost jerked the buggy's wheels clear of the ground as they started it moving. Dusty thought back with gratitude to buggyraces between the Regiment's young officers. From them he learned how to handle a fast-moving vehicle and pair of team horses. That knowledge came in very useful as he guided the carriage away. Although the two cavalrymen gave chase, on foot they stood little chance of keeping up with the speeding carriage and neither thought to use their guns.

"Keep going, Dusty!" Belle said. "We've got to get away."

CHAPTER NINE

A Dress for an Engineer's Wife

While the two cavalrymen fell behind, they still kept up the chase and in doing so attracted the attention of other soldiers. Holding the two horses to a fast gallop along the centre of a street, Dusty saw a man dart from the sidewalk in an attempt to catch hold of the reins. Taking up the carriage whip from its holder, Dusty sent the lash slicing forward. For a snap shot he aimed well and the leather curled about the man's head, causing an immediate withdrawal.

Seeing what happened to the soldier, a second man tried a different method of halting the carriage. Racing forward, he came in behind and grabbed hold of the rear of the passengers' seat. Only he failed to take one thing into account and his plan met with a check. Rising up before the surprised man, Belle lashed around her right fist in a punch which snapped his head to one side and caused him to lose his hold. Before the man landed on the street, Dusty started to swing the racing carriage around another corner.

Shouts rang out, whistles blew and hooves clattered as

members of the Provost Marshal's mounted patrol headed for the disturbance area. Luck favoured Belle and Dusty for none of the riders came their way. However they realised that they must leave the carriage at the first favourable opportunity. It did not come for some time and the sound of pursuit kept at about the same distance behind them. Sensing trouble, the citizens disappeared into their homes, or entered business premises, with the intention of disassociating themselves and so as to be unable to help the Yankees should they be asked.

Swinging the horses on to a street which ran behind big buildings that in time of peace housed businessmen, or supplied town homes for plantation owners, Dusty saw his chance. Nobody appeared to be watching them and their pursuers had not yet come into sight. So Dusty hauled back on the reins and slowed the carriage.

"Get out, Belle!" he snapped.

Bag in hand, the girl obeyed. She thrust open the carriage door, paused to catch her balance and leapt down. Lashing the reins on to the whip, which he had thrust back into its holder, Dusty rose on the seat. He let out another yell, which caused the horses to lunge forward into the harness once more and start running, then sprang clear. As Dusty lit down on the sidewalk, the carriage tore away along the street.

"Down there, Dusty," Belle suggested, darting to the small Texan's side.

Flights of steps ran down into small areas that opened into the houses' basement kitchens and Belle led the way out of sight. No sooner had they gone than feet clattered, hooves drummed and some of their pursuers turned on to the street. Gun in hand, Dusty flattened himself by Belle against the area wall and listened to their hunters pass them.

"So far, so good," Dusty breathed. "Only we'd best find some better place than this to hide afore they find that buggy's empty."

"Let's see if we can get into the house. Most of them are empty, their owners went up river when the Yankees came," Belle replied, walking to the door and reaching for its handle. "This's probably a waste of time—Hey, it's not."

At Belle's turn of the handle and push, the door swung inwards. Followed by Dusty, the girl entered a kitchen, that, before the War, would have held several servants. Only a pair of elderly Negroes stood in the room, the man reaching for a butcher's knife on the table at which they stood.

"Put it down and keep quiet, friend," Dusty said quietly, holding his Colt but not threatening the man.

"What do you want, mister?" the man asked, still holding the knife.

Before Dusty could answer, an old white woman entered the kitchen. Despite her faded old clothes, she still retained an air of breeding. Tall, slim, the woman stood studying the newcomers and her face showed no fear.

"What is it, Sam?" she asked.

"Don't be frightened, ma'am," Dusty told her.

"I wasn't aware of being frightened, young man," she answered. "May I ask what brings you here. And put that gun away. This isn't Texas and you won't need it."

Clearly the old woman recognised a Texas drawl when she heard one. Her eyes darted from Dusty, as he returned the Colt to his waistband, to Belle. The girl spoke up.

"We're in trouble, ma'am."

"*That* strikes me as being obvious. Come here, girl, and show me your hands."

Flashing a smile at Dusty, Belle crossed the room towards the old woman. The small Texan remained at the door, holding it open a little so as to watch and listen to the noises in the street. With her hands held out like when, as a child, she stood inspection before going in to meet the guests at a tea party, Belle allowed the woman to scrutinise her carefully. Then the old woman glanced at the bag and ledger Belle set down on the table before showing her hands.

"You're dressed as a maid," the woman remarked. "But you've a lady's hands and voice. A lady and a Texan who's obviously a soldier and doesn't look like the kind to be a deserter. I may say that you two interest me. Just what are the Yankees after you for?"

"Robbing a shop and shooting a man in it," Belle replied.

"Killing him?"

"Possibly."

"Was he the owner?" demanded the old woman, a different note coming into her voice and a glint flickering in her eyes.

"No," Belle answered. "I believe he was one of Pinkerton's men."

"A member of the Yankee Secret Service?"

"He certainly didn't work for Madam Lucienne."

"Is that why you took the ledger?"

Belle nodded agreement. Realising that she stood in the presence of a very shrewd, discerning woman, she decided to tell the truth. Unless Belle missed her guess, she could rely on the woman's loyalty to the South and need not be afraid to disclose her identity.

"My name is Boyd—," she began.

"One of the Baton Royale Boyds?" asked the woman.

"My father was Vincent Boyd of Baton Royale," Belle admitted.

"Who had only one daughter, Belle by name. Belle Boyd, who is also known as the Rebel Spy."

"That's what they call me. Although I doubt if the Yankees know it's me they are hunting."

"Then they won't search so thoroughly," guessed the old woman, directing an inquiring glance in Dusty's direction.

"May I introduce Captain Dusty Fog?" Belle said. "He is assisting me on my present assignment."

"My pleasure, ma'am," Dusty drawled, closing the door and crossing the room.

Even in occupied New Orleans Dusty's fame had spread amongst the Southerners and the old woman beamed delightedly. However she did not allow her pleasure at meeting Dusty to interfere with the business on hand.

"It may be as well if you go and hide in case a search is made," she stated.

"How about your servants, ma'am?" asked Dusty.

"You can trust Sam and Jessie as you trust me," she answered. "Come along."

Leading Belle and Dusty into what had once been a comfortable study, but which showed signs of having various furnishings removed, the woman—she introduced herself as Mrs. Annie Rowley—supplied them with a very good place of concealment. At times members of many New Orleans families found the need to keep out of sight for a few days: maybe to avoid somebody wishing to issue a challenge; or, when duelling became illegal, to hide after a duel until a suitable arrangement could be made with the court to overlook the matter. Clearly the Rowleys belonged to that class, for the old woman operated a disguised switch and a section of wall pannelling slid back to reveal a small, comfortable and ventilated room.

"Go in. I'll have food brought for you," she said.

Dusty and Belle exchanged glances as the same thought ran through their heads. Life in the occupied city could not be easy for Mrs. Rowley. Too old to work, her normal sources of revenue taken by the War, she clearly had to sell items of her property to support herself. So feeding two extra people would create a serious drain in her resources. Yet she might take offence at any offer of payment. Receiving a nod of agreement from Belle, Dusty took a chance.

"May we offer to help pay for the meal, ma'am?" he asked.

"I would like a lemon if one can be bought," Belle went on.

"There was a time when your offer would have offended me," Mrs. Rowly admitted. "But I'm afraid the War caused many things to change in my life—."

"This's stolen money," Dusty warned with a grin as he started to empty his pockets.

"I thought 'booty' was the term when it's taken from the enemy in time of war," smiled the woman. "It'll spend well enough at the market no matter what we chose to call it."

"Can your servants raise a lemon?" Belle asked.

"Land-sakes, girl," Mrs. Rowley answered. "That's a strange fancy. There are lemons for sale, I'll have Jessie bring some."

"Only one," Belle corrected.

"I'll tell Jessie," promised Mrs. Rowly. "Now you two had best hide."

Like most of its kind, the secret room offered reasonable comfort in the shape of a bed, table and chair. Entering, Dusty and Belle watched the door start to swing shut behind them. Then Dusty rasped a match on his pants' seat and lit the lamp on the table. With a sigh Belle stretched on the bed, the ledger and bag at its side. She glanced at the closed door, then to Dusty.

"Well," she said. "Have we made a mistake?"

"We're caught in a box canyon if we have," he answered, thinking how much the Yankees would pay for the capture of the Rebel Spy and himself. Taking a small box from his pocket, he opened it to expose twelve combustible cartridges and a similar number of percussion caps. "I'll fit that empty chamber just in case. Then we'll grab some rest."

Neither really thought the old woman would betray them and were fatalistic enough to realise they could do nothing but wait to find out. So, after Dusty replaced the discharged round and put out the lamp, they settled down to rest. Neither had any idea how long they lay in the darkness, Dusty seated on the chair with his boots on the table and Belle on the bed. At last they heard a creaking and the door began to inch slowly open.

Gun in hand, Dusty came to his feet and Belle rolled from the bed gripping her Dance ready for use. Then both knew they did not need to fear treachery. Slowly the door continued to open, allowing light to creep gradually into the room in a manner which permitted their eyes to grow accustomed to no longer being in complete darkness. If there had been a betrayal, the enemy would just jerk open the door and move in while the sudden advent of light dazzled the pair inside.

"It's all clear now," Mrs. Rowley said, smiling in at them.

"Did the Yankees come?" asked Belle, returning her Dance to the bag.

"Came and searched the house, then went away satisfied," replied the old woman. "From what their sergeant said, it's assumed that you're just ordinary thieves and slipped back to the waterfront area. He didn't hold out much hope of finding you."

"The two men at the shop couldn't have talked yet then," Dusty commented. "Likely the one I shot can't and it'll be a spell afore the other's able to, the way you slammed him into the wall, Belle."

"I've a meal ready for you, and your lemon," the woman told them. "And Sam's watching the street in case the Yankees come back."

After eating a good meal, Belle took her bag and ledger to the table and started to work. From the bag she lifted her jewel case and extracted the brooch which held the lens. With it she examined each unused page of the book. To do so she stood by a window and allowed the light of the afternoon sun to fall on the paper. The lemon had not been bought for eating purposes and its use soon became apparent.

"I can't find any traces of pen-scratches," she said at last. "But I'll try the usual tests."

"You figure Madam Lucienne used invisible ink?" asked an interested Dusty.

"She left information in the ledger some way," the girl replied. "We use two kinds of invisible ink. One appears when you apply lemon juice to the paper and heat produces the other."

Although both tests were tried on various pages, no writing appeared and at last Belle reluctantly admitted that however Madam Lucienne left her message, invisible ink had not been used.

"Could be inside the ledger's bindings," Dusty suggested.

"It could be," admitted Belle. "Could we have a knife, please Mrs. Rowley."

"Of course," answered the old woman, having been an interested spectator.

Carefully Belle slit open the leather binding of the ledger, checking its inner side and the stiffeners without result.

"Nothing," she said. "Yet Madam Lucienne told me the information was in it."

"She might have written a message in among the other writing in it," Dusty offered.

"It's possible," the girl said. "Let's try and see."

Turning to the first page, Belle started to read. She tried taking the first letter of each order, but they made no sense. Then something caught her eye. Somebody in Baton Royale had bought a ball gown, a person she had never heard of and at a plantation which Belle could not recall. Yet the name did not help her any nor the address and she cursed the bad luck which prevented Madam Lucienne from being able to give her more information when they met; the meeting had been terminated by the arrival of a Yankee naval captain and his wife at the shop.

After the failure with the address, Belle read on to learn how a Mrs. J. Bludso of the Busted Boiler Inn in New Orleans bought a silk ball gown. Finishing the page, Belle turned over no wiser than when she began. Nor did enlightenment come until three more pages went by. Suddenly the girl stopped, sat staring thoughtfully at the ledger for a moment and then turned back to the first page.

"Something, Belle?" Dusty asked.

"Listen to this and tell me what you think," she answered. "One silk ball gown for Mrs. J. Bludso, the Busted Boiler Inn, price twenty-five dollars."

"So?"

"On the next page the order is repeated and on the third."

"You said Madam Lucienne was mighty popular," Dusty pointed out. "Likely a woman'd keep going to her if she got good service."

"Three times in less than two months?" Belle replied.

"I would for bargains like that," Mrs. Rowley put in. "You show me any place that can supply a silk ball gown for twenty-five dollars."

"If I find one, I'll keep quiet about it, buy some and make a fortune," smiled Belle. "The Busted Boiler's in the waterfront district; it's, or used to be, the gathering place for the riverboat engineers."

"And young Jim Bludso was engineer of the Prairie Belle," Mrs. Rowley recalled. "Only she went down trying to ram one of Farragut's gunboats before the surrender. I know engineers made good money, but not enough for one to shop regularly at Madam Lucienne's."

"This's what we want, Dusty," Belle stated. "It must be."

"She'd be taking a big chance putting it down that way," Dusty objected.

"Not so big," Belle replied. "I doubt if a man would see any significance in the entries. I might not have but for that false address in Baton Royale above the first mention of Mrs. J. Bludso."

"What're we going to do then?" Dusty asked.

"Go to the Busted Boiler and see Jim Bludso," the girl replied.

"Do you know it?" asked Mrs. Rowley.

"We can find it," Belle answered.

"Wait until after dark and I'll send Sam to guide you," the woman suggested. "It's little enough I can do for the South, so don't argue."

Accompanied by the old Negro, Belle and Dusty passed through the evening-darkened streets. Clearly the Yankees attached little importance to their visit to Madam Lucienne's shop, for only normal patrols moved through the streets. Even if the two men should be dead, the military authorities most likely took the attitude that the killers had disappeared into the city and organising a search capable of producing results would take more men than they had available. Whatever the reason, none of the patrols met during the journey gave Belle, Dusty and the Negro more than a casual glance in passing.

At last Sam halted. They had long since left the elegant area behind and walked through streets which grew narrower, dirtier, more crowded. Much of the atmosphere of the waterfront departed with the city's surrender. In times of peace the area boomed with unceasing life and gaiety, as wild and hectic as in any gold camp or—in later years— town at the end of the long cattle drives from Texas to Kansas. Many of the saloons, dance or gambling halls and other places of business were closed, but some remained open in the hope of grabbing trade from the U.S. forces.

The Busted Boiler was a small hotel set back off a street facing the river and comprised of businesses concerned with the riverboat trade. At one time it served as a gathering point for most of the riverboats' engineers; and there had been sufficient of them to ensure the owner a steady custom. After directing his companions to the place, Sam disappeared into the darkness and they walked towards its doors. In passing they glanced through the windows at the right of the door and did not like what they saw. Yankee sailors and marines sat around the dining room, or leaned at the bar. Only a few civilians were present, mingling with the uniformed men and apparently on good terms with them. At a table in the centre of the room, a big, wide-shouldered man whose curly black hair showed from under a pushed-back peaked civilian seaman's hat sat dining with a trio of U.S. Navy petty officers and clearly all enjoyed their meal.

"What about it?" Dusty asked.

"I don't know," Belle replied. "Stay out here and cover me while I go ask for Bludso."

"Are you taking your bag?"

"No—but I'll take the parasol."

After assembling the parasol into its harmless form, Belle

left her bag in Dusty's keeping and entered the hotel. The arrival of a woman attracted no especial attention, although Belle saw men studying her with interest. Then a bulky Negress waitress came to a halt before the girl.

"You wanted something?"

"Is Jim Bludso here?" Belle inquired.

"He sure am, gal," grinned the Negress. "Does you-all want him?"

"I'm his sister," Belle replied.

"Ain't dey all, gal?" asked the Negress and ambled away.

Crossing the room, the Negress halted by the big civilian with the three petty officers. A puzzled expression flickered across his face as the woman spoke and indicated Belle. One of the petty officers made a comment and his companions laughed, then the civilian rose and walked in Belle's direction.

Studying the man, Belle formed an impression of strength, toughness and capability. He wore a short coat, open-necked shirt, trousers tucked into sea-boots and a long-bladed knife hung sheathed at his left side. Good-looking in a rugged, tanned way, he grinned as he drew near.

"Why howdy," he greeted. "Are you-all a sister on my mammy or pappy's side?"

"Why Jim," Belle replied. "Pappy's for sure. He told me to come here and speak to you about your extravagant ways. Three silk ball gowns for your wife, for shame."

If the words carried any special meaning to the big man, he gave no sign of it. The smile never left his lips and he took the girl's right arm in his big left hand. Gently but firmly he turned her towards the door.

"Let's us go someplace quiet where we can talk about it," he suggested.

"Why I just adore big strong men," Belle purred. "But I don't need force—"

"You keep walking like we the best of friends, gal," Jim Bludso ordered. "If you don't, I'll bust your arm."

Belle carried the parasol in her left hand, but did not

offer to take it apart as a means of defending herself. To do so in the hotel invited capture. Once outside, she and Dusty between them ought to be able to handle Jim Bludso. Unresisting, she allowed herself to be steered towards the front door.

CHAPTER TEN

Another Talented Lady

With Bludso retaining a grip on her arm, Belle left the hotel. She darted a glance in either direction as she walked through the door, but could see no sign of Dusty. Wondering where the small Texan might be, she allowed Bludso to steer her along the sidewalk and into the alley at the left side of the building.

"Just what's the game?" she demanded, realising that she ought to be saying or doing something.

"What do you know about those ball gowns?" Bludso countered, not relaxing his grip.

"Only what Madam Lucienne wanted me to know."

"Who're you?"

"Would you believe me if I said I was her dress designer?"

"No—," Bludso began.

At that moment he heard a soft footfall behind him. So did Belle, but with a difference—she could guess at who approached quietly from behind them. Even as Bludso sent his left hand towards the hilt of the knife he wore, Belle

made her play. With Dusty so close at hand, she decided
not to release her skirt. Although retaining the garment
lessened the methods by which she could defend herself,
she felt adequate to the present situation.

Raising her left leg, Belle stamped backwards to drive
the heel of her shoe hard against Bludso's left shin. A croak
of pain broke from his lips and he involuntarily loosened
his hold on the girl's arm. With a heave Belle freed herself
and shot her elbow back to collide with Bludso's solar plexus.
Taken unawares by the attack, Bludso rocked back and
struck the wall. A tough, hard man—riverboat life did not
breed weaklings—he threw off the effects of Belle's stamp
and blow fast; the recovery might not have been so speedy
if the girl used her full power. Before Bludso could make
a move, Dusty stood before him with a lined Army Colt.

"Hold it right there, mister," the small Texan ordered
and the cocking click of the gun added its backing to the
command.

Bludso was no fool. Maybe he lacked a comprehensive
knowledge of gunfighters' ways, but he knew enough to
recognise top class work when he saw it. Small the man
before him might be, but he handled the Colt with a casual,
assured ease that told of long practice. From his voice, he
hailed out of Texas and the Lone Star State had already
begun to build its reputation for producing skilled revolver-
handling men. Significantly the small Texan stood just close
enough to ensure a hit, but too far away to allow a successful
grab by Bludso at his weapon.

In addition Bludso could not overlook the manner in
which the girl defended herself. Not in panic, but with
deadly, skilled purpose and just at the right moment when
his attention was divided between her and the approaching
man.

"Southrons hear your country call you," Belle said quietly.

"Up lest worse than death befall you," Bludso replied,
feeling just a touch relieved at the familiar password. "Why

didn't you say you were one of us?"

"You never gave me a chance," Belle pointed out. "I think they've got Madam Lucienne. There were two of Pinkerton's spies at the shop when we arrived."

"So it was you pair who downed Turnpike and Kaddam," Bludso said. "Come with me, this's not the place for us to stand talking."

With that Bludso turned and walked through the alley towards the rear. He showed such complete trust that Dusty and Belle did not hesitate to follow. At the back of the hotel a flight of stairs ran up to a first floor room and Bludso began to climb them. Not until then did Belle request advice.

"Where're we going?" she asked.

"This's where I live and I can't think of a better place for us to talk," Bludso answered. "It's better we go this way than through the front door. Those Yankee brass-pounders're used to me meeting gals, but not when the gal has a feller along with her."

"It's your play," Dusty stated.

At the top of the stairs Bludso opened his room's door and walked straight in. Deciding that the man probably did not need to use correct manners with his normal run of lady-friends, Belle followed and Dusty brought up the rear. As soon as they entered the room, its door slammed behind them and a lantern's light burst out from under cover. Dusty cursed, bringing up his gun, but was so dazzled by the sudden light that he could not see anything more than a milky-white blur. Nor did Belle fare any better. Dusty carried her bag in his left hand, which allowed her to jerk the head from her parasol and free its deadly billy. Armed in that way, she still could barely see enough to use the billy. Clearly Bludso expected the light. On entering, he must have kept his eyes closed and avoided the main impact of the glare. Out came his knife and he dropped easily into a knifefighter's crouch. Facing Dusty and Belle, he darted a glance at the woman who stood holding a bucket with which she had covered the lighted lantern until it was required.

"You sure fell for that one, Belle gal," the woman said with a broad grin.

"Don't shoot, Dusty!" warned Belle, recognising the voice.

When Dusty's eyes cleared, he saw a plump, jovial-looking woman with hair that retained its red tint through liberal use of henna dye. Even clad in a cheap dress such as a woman of the dock-area might wear, she gave off an air of theatrical leanings and looked as if she played a part rather than belonged to the district.

"You know them, Lucy?" asked Bludso.

"Not the feller, but the girl is Belle Boyd."

"So you're safe after all, Lucienne," Belle said, reassembling her parasol.

"Sure," Madam Lucienne replied. "I see you worked out where to come from my ledger. I didn't have time to take it with me when I lit out."

"Sorry, Miss Boyd," Bludso said, sheathing his knife. "I didn't know who you might be and wasn't in a position to raise the question. So I figured that it'd be best to get you up here where Lucy and me could tend to your needings. Let's get sat down, in case I have callers."

Sitting around the table, the quartet got down to business. After Dusty had been introduced, Madam Lucienne told how she escaped from the two Yankee agents.

"I don't know how they found out about me," she said, "but I recognised one of them and pulled out the back when they came in at the front. I came down here, changed and have been with Jim from this morning. We aimed to see if we could get into the shop and collect the ledger tonight."

"We've saved you that chore," Belle told her. "Is there anything else of importance in the shop?"

"Nothing that they can find, or would help them if they did," Lucienne replied. "I never kept written records if I could help it and all my other gear's safe. What brings you and Captain Fog into New Orleans, Belle?"

"Something really important," the girl replied, darting a glance at Bludso. "How do you fit into this?"

"Jim and I work together," Lucienne explained. "He passes on the information our folks gather when he goes up river."

"The Yankees need good engineers," Bludso went on. "I'm one of the best and they can trust me. I've helped keep some of their boats working——."

"After he and his men damaged them in the first place," grinned Lucienne. "So you can trust Jim all the way."

"Of course," smiled Belle.

"I don't trust folks on face value either," Bludso said with a grin. "Which you may have noticed."

Which put the meeting on a friendly basis again. Bludso, being a cautious man, did not object to Belle showing the same traits. Both worked in a business where the penalty for failure was death, and had learned early not to take any unnecessary chances.

Quickly Belle told of the discovery made in Arkansas and explained the serious threat posed by the conterfeiting for Bludso's benefit. Soon the engineer's face set in grim lines and he nodded his head.

"We'll have to stop it," he stated. "Thing now being, how to do it."

"We'll have to raid Gaton's place," Dusty said. "Only before we do it, I'd admire to know what force he has guarding it. We may need help."

"That I can supply," Bludso replied. "And I can fix it to learn all we need to know about Gaton's guards. Got the combustibles we'll need stashed away, too."

"Do you have a man who knows how to break open a safe?" asked Belle.

"I don't reckon so," admitted Bludso.

"That's where I can help," Lucienne put in. "I can take you to a man who'll supply a safe-breaker for a price."

"I've five hundred dollars in gold in my bag," Belle told her. "Will that be enough?"

"If not, we've our own supply to back you," Lucienne replied. "While Jim learns all he can about Gaton's place, you, Dusty and me will go visit this feller."

"Who is he?" Belle asked.

"Harwold Cornwall."

From the way Lucienne merely said the name, she concluded it to be enough and ought to tell the others all that was necessary. The name meant nothing to Dusty, although the time would come when he took an interest in the affairs of Harwold Cornwall.* Certainly he was the only one present who did not know the man named.

"Hell, Lucy!" Bludso burst out. "You can't take a lady like Miss Boyd into Cornwall's place."

"Can we trust him?" Belle asked, ignoring the man's comment.

"About as far as you could throw a bull by the tail," Lucienne replied. "But if the price's right he will do what he can for us."

"You have to excuse a half-smart lil country boy like me," Dusty drawled. "But just who is this Cornwall *hombre?*"

"A thief," growled Bludso.

"And just about the biggest in New Orleans," Lucienne went on. "He's smarter than most and the law's never proved a thing against him. But he's behind most of the law-breaking in the city."

"Most of his kind got out before the Yankees arrived," Bludso continued. "I reckon they thought there wouldn't be any pickings."

"Not Cornwall though," Lucienne finished. "He runs a place called the Green Peacock not far from here. It's real popular with the Yankees."

"And you figure *he'll* help us?" asked Dusty.

"If the price's right he will," Lucienne agreed. "Not that we'll let him know why we want the safe-breaker. If he

Told in "The Man from Texas."

learns later, he won't dare open his mouth about it. Anyway, I know enough about Cornwall to keep him quiet."

"Let's go then," Belle suggested. "We've only three days to handle this business."

"Why the rush?" Bludso inquired.

"A submersible is coming to pick us up three nights from now. So we'll have to move real fast."

"We'd best start right away then," Lucienne stated. "You see to your end of it, Jim. I'll take Belle and Dusty to see Cornwall."

"Will it be safe for you to walk through the streets, Lucienne?" asked Dusty. "With the Yankees looking for you and all."

"A change of clothing and hair-style's all I need," the woman assured him. "And I've had both of them here. Don't forget that it was mostly the wives of the Yankee officers who knew me—and there'll be none of *them* where we're going."

"How about the pair we had a run-in with at your place?" Dusty went on.

"From what I heard, neither of them are in any shape to be walking the streets tonight," Lucienne answered.

"We have to take that chance anyway, Dusty," Belle warned. "Lucienne can deal with Cornwall better than either of us."

"That's for sure," agreed Lucienne. "I talk his language, Dusty. Come on, Belle. We'll go to my room and fix ourselves up."

"Something more suitable in clothing is definitely called for," the girl admitted, running a hand down her dress.

Watching the girl leave, Dusty wondered what she intended to change into. Certainly the travelling suit would not fit into the scene at a fancy New Orleans saloon any more than the maid's outfit.

While waiting for the women to return, Dusty and Bludso talked. Although the big man could shed no light on Lucienne's past, or guess how she might know a man like

Harwold Cornwall, he seemed certain that she could gain the criminal's co-operation. In the course of their conversation, Bludso admitted that he knew of the secret submersible dock, but did not blame Belle for her reticence on the matter. He also seemed just as sure that he could learn all they would need to know about the lay-out and personnel at Gaton's house.

"My striker off the old Prairie Belle'll do it," Bludso stated confidently. "Old Willie's real slick at learning things."

"How about the combustibles?" Dusty asked.

"We've all we need in a safe place."

"Best not make plans until we know exactly what we'll need, though, Jim."

"Nope. But I can raise all the men we might want at short notice."

After that the conversation turned to more general matters; the progress of the War in the East and Arkansas was discussed, then Bludso spoke of conditions in occupied New Orleans.

At last the door opened and the women entered. Used as he had become to the way in which Belle could change her appearance, Dusty still stared hard at what he saw. To the best of his knowledge, the girl brought along only two dresses and the male clothing. Yet she walked into Bludso's room clad in a manner more suited to a saloongirl than a travelling lady or a maid.

A blonde wig replaced the other and her beautiful face carried stage make-up like any saloongirl's. Although she wore a black skirt still, it clung tighter to her and glinted flashily instead of being drab. Above the skirt, a sleeveless white satin blouse hugged her torso, left her shoulders bare and its decollete was cut low enough to allow the valley between her breasts to show. Despite its excellent quality, the jewellery she wore looked cheap and flashy when taken with her general appearance. Nor did the deadly parasol look out of place.

"Well?" she asked.

"That'd really make Uncle Devil bristle," Dusty grinned. "How'd you do it?"

"Turned the skirt inside out and tightened it," the girl explained. "Took the sleeves and part of the top off my blouse and turned it inside out too. Will it do, Dusty?"

"Do? I wouldn't know you if I'd seen you passing in the street," Dusty enthused. "Do all women's clothes have such fancy fittings?"

"No," Belle replied, then nodded in Madam Lucienne's direction. "But I have a very smart seamstress."

"I'll be the last to deny that," grinned the woman.

Turning his attention to Lucienne, Dusty realised that he stood in the presence of yet another talented lady. In addition to being able to design clothes ideally suited to a female spy's specialised needs, Lucienne proved to be almost Belle's equal at changing her appearance. She too now looked like the kind of woman who frequented saloons, with her hair and dress changed so that they met the required state. In fact both she and Belle looked so different that Dusty could understand their confidence at not being recognised.

At the corner of the Busted Boiler, Bludso left Belle, Lucienne and Dusty and went to organise his part of the business. The trio walked along behind the buildings for a time and then came out on to the street. With Lucienne guiding them, they passed quickly through what had been the centre of better-class waterfront entertainment before the War. Even with the Yankees in occupation several saloons remained open and drew trade.

The Green Peacock proved to be the biggest, best and most popular place on the street. In fact it drew such a volume of business that Dusty wondered if some special entertainment brought in the crowd. Music blared from a tolerably good band, mingling with laughter, droning conversation and the clatter of glasses. Naturally the majority of the customers wore Federal uniforms, although some civilians were present. Clearly the saloon rated highly, for Yankee Army, Navy and Marine personnel of various ranks gathered in it.

In the centre of the room stood a raised wooden platform, square in shape and with an upright post at each corner supporting two tight ropes which stretched all the way around. Dusty recognised the construction as a 'ring' of the kind used to stage fist fights. While the Texas Light Cavalry preferred more basic methods of settling their differences, or laid their sporting emphasis on events involving the use of horse or gun, a near-by Confederate infantry regiment went in for pugilism and often held prize fights to relieve their boredom between spells of active service.

Knowing that prize fights often were staged by saloon-keepers, Dusty wondered if the crowd gathered that night to witness one of exceptional merit.

At first nobody took any notice of the trio's entrance. Then a passing waiter threw a glance their way and came to a halt.

"You bunch wanting something?"

"We've come to see Harwold Cornwall," Lucienne replied.

"Looking for work?" asked the man.

"Could be," she answered. "Tell him that it's Auntie Buckhalter wants a word in private."

"I'll tell him," sniffed the waiter. "Only he's entertaining a couple of Yankee Navy captains and likely won't see you."

"You've a big surprise coming," smiled Lucienne as the man walked away to deliver the order he carried before passing on her message.

"I tell you it's the same girl!" declared a voice from a table close to where the trio stood. "It's Jim Bludso's 'sister.'"

Turning her head slightly, Belle saw Bludso's three companions from the Busted Boiler. They sat entertaining a trio of the saloon's girls and the tallest of them pointed straight at her.

"That one was a lady's maid and not a blonde," a second man objected.

"I tell you that's her," the first insisted.

His voice carried to more than Belle's ears. Swinging around in her seat at the next table, a stocky brunette glared first at the speaker, then in Belle's direction. At the brunette's side, a sharp-faced little man spoke quietly but urgently in her ear. Ignoring the man, the brunette thrust back her chair, rose and stalked grimly towards the slim girl. Halting on spread-apart feet and with arms akimbo on her hips, the brunette looked Belle up and down with cold eyes.

"Have you been hanging around Jim Bludso?" the brunette demanded.

Almost as tall as Belle, the woman weighed heavier, was reasonably good-looking and showed hard muscles on her bent arms. In view of the question, and recalling the comment of the Negress at the Busted Boiler when she asked for Bludso, Belle could have groaned. The last thing she wanted was to have trouble with another of Jim Bludso's 'sisters' and it seemed the brunette belonged to that class. Fortunately at that moment a troop of acrobats appeared on the stage and drew the attention of most of the room's occupants in that direction.

Most, but not all. The trio of petty officers watched the two women and exchanged knowing grins.

"I don't know what you mean," Belle said meekly.

"Was she the one, sailor?" the brunette asked, glancing at the tallest of the trio.

Even then trouble might have been averted, but the petty officer had no wish for it to be. Flickering another knowing leer at his companions, he nodded his head.

"It sure was," he stated. "A man wouldn't forget one of old Jim's 'sisters' who's that pretty."

Turning a cold, angry face to Belle once more, the brunette hissed, "I've warned you lobby-lizzies* to steer clear of Jim Bludso. When I've done with you, there won't be so many of you wanting to bother him."

With that the brunette laid her right hand on Belle's bust

*Lobby-Lizzy: A prostitute.

and shoved her. Even as Belle struck the wall, she saw the woman draw back and drive out a clenched left fist. Noting the skilled manner in which the brunette acted, Belle knew she could take no chances. Especially against a woman as strong and capable as the other showed herself.

Just before the fist reached her face, Belle ducked and swayed aside. She timed the move right, allowing no opportunity for the brunette to halt the blow. Hissing harmlessly by the girl's head, the brunette's hand smashed with sickening force into the wall. A squeal of pain broke from the woman's lips and Belle held back the punch she automatically prepared to launch. Gripping her injured hand, the woman tottered backwards.

"Ruby!" yelped the little man, having watched every move. Concern showed on his face as he sprang forward. "Let me see that hand."

"Leave it, Belle!" Lucienne snapped, catching the girl's arm.

"I want to see if she's badly hurt," Belle objected.

"The waiter's coming back," Lucienne replied. "Forget her, she asked for it."

CHAPTER ELEVEN

The Price for Cornwall's Aid

Comparatively few of the crowd witnessed the incident. Seeing the brunette sink to her knees, moaning and cradling the damaged hand, those who saw decided that the scene possessed no further dramatic possibilities, so turned their attention to the acrobats on the stage.

"The boss'll see you in his office," announced the waiter as he came up, showing more respect than on their arrival. Then he darted a glance at the injured brunette and a startled expression crossed his face. "What happened to Ruby?"

"She ran into the wall," Lucienne replied calmly. "Let's go see Cornwall, shall we?"

Looking to where the waiter came from, Dusty saw a tall, well-dressed man rise from a table shared with two Yankee Navy captains and walk in the direction of a door marked 'Private.' A big, heavily-built hard-case moved across the room in the man's direction, swerved off as if at a signal and lounged casually shoulder on the wall and back towards the door.

Standing behind his desk in the office, Harwold Cornwall looked at the trio as they entered. He gave most of his attention to Lucienne, staring hard at her face. At last a hint of recognition came to his hard, heavily moustached features.

"I heard you'd died, Annie," he said. "Who're the other two?"

"Friends of mine. I need your help, Harwold."

Before any more could be said, a knock sounded at the door and the waiter entered. Dusty stepped by Lucienne and halted alongside Cornwall's side of the desk as the door opened, but made no move. Scowling at the waiter, Cornwall growled that he left word not to be disturbed.

"Wilf wants to see you real important, boss," the waiter replied and the brunette's companion came into the office, crossing to the desk.

"What's up, Wilf?" Cornwall demanded.

Leaning across the desk, the man spoke in a low voice. A soft curse broke from Cornwall's lips and he threw a furious glare in Belle's direction. Then he listened again to the small man and made a reply too low for Dusty, Belle or Lucienne to catch. Straightening up, the man turned and walked towards the door. Dusty saw Cornwall nod meaningfully to the waiter, who followed the man out.

"You've put me in a hell of a fix, Annie," Cornwall remarked in a friendly tone and drew open his desk's drawer. "And I reckon you should—."

Fooled by Dusty's insignificant appearance, Cornwall failed to regard him as a factor in the affair. Too late the saloonkeeper learned his mistake. Like a flash Dusty's right hand disappeared under the left side of his jacket and came out holding the Army Colt. Although he could not produce his full, blinding speed when working from the waistband, the Colt still made its appearance in a manner amazingly fast to eyes unused to range-country gun-handling. Certainly Cornwall had never seen anything so fast and his first intimation of danger came when the cold muzzle of the Colt touched his ear. The shock caused him to jerk his hand away from the open drawer. He sat as if turned to stone, ignoring the Adams Navy revolver scant inches beneath his fingers.

Down swooped Dusty's left hand, taking out the Adams. He tossed it to Belle without taking his Colt away from Cornwall's ear. Deftly catching the Adams by its butt, Belle swung to face the door and covered the burly hard-case as he entered. The man came to a halt, staring from Belle to Cornwall as if in search of instructions. Receiving none, the hard-case wisely stood still.

"What's gnawing at you, Harwold?" Lucienne asked.

"Do you know who your gal crippled out there?" he countered.

"No," Lucienne answered. "Put up the guns, you two."

"It was Ruby Toot," Cornwall explained, signalling for his man to leave.

"And who's she?" Lucienne inquired, her companions leaving her to speak for them. With the man gone, Dusty slid away his Colt and Belle returned the Adams.

"Just the gal who was going to fight English Flo tonight," Cornwall growled.

"Fight her?" Lucienne repeated.

"In the ring, Annie. The customers got tired of seeing male pugilists, so I put English Flo and another gal in one night. When I saw how they went for it, I started training up more gals. So did Ross down the street. Ruby Toot's his best gal and we fixed the match for her against English Flo. There'll be all hell pop if I have to tell that crowd the fight's off."

"I'm sorry about it, Harwold," Lucienne stated. "But the big gal laid into Becky here first."

"You didn't know anything about this then?"

"No."

"There's been a lot of money bet against Flo. I thought maybe—."

"No. I didn't bring Becky here to get that gal hurt so the bets will be called off," Lucienne said. "I came here to ask you to find me a safe-breaker in a real hurry."

"Can I ask why?"

"I know where I can pick up some Yankee gold, Harwold. The War ruined my business and I've been lying low watching for this chance. Now I know where I can make enough for a fresh start."

"Here in New Orleans?" asked Cornwall, his tone indicating that the prospect would not please him.

"No. Out in California. Can you get the man I want tonight?"

"Maybe—for a price."

"How much?"

"Not much. I want a replacement for Ruby Toot."

Although she knew what Cornwall was driving at, Lucienne asked, "How do you mean, Harwold?"

"Wilf told me how your girl handled herself against Ruby. If you taught her, she can take care of herself. Put her against Flo and I'll find the man you want."

"Like he—!" began Dusty.

"How much money, Harwold?" interrupted Lucienne.

"No money. The gal fights, or no help."

"All right," Belle put in quietly. "I'll do it."

A grin creased the saloonkeeper's face as he studied the girl. Most likely she could put up a reasonable show, and her good looks would distract the crowd, while English Flo should beat her easily.

"It's on then, Harwold," Lucienne declared, throwing a warning glance at Dusty. "Becky'll be ready to fight *when* you get the feller here. I want to be sure he's worth her trouble."

"Hell!" Cornwall snorted. "I'm not sure how long it'll take to find a good safe man."

"Then start looking!" Lucienne snapped. "When I've seen the feller and made my deal, Becky'll go out there and fight."

"I'll see what I can do," Cornwall growled. "And I'll

see about fixing your girl up with some clothes. She can't go into the ring in that dress."

"If you don't find a safe man, don't bother," Lucienne said calmly. "And no tricks, Harwold. I know things about you the Yankees'd be pleased to hear."

"Such as?"

Leaning across the desk, Lucienne whispered in the man's ear. Whatever she told him, the effect proved satisfactory. An expression of shocked anger crossed the man's face and he opened his mouth to ask a question, but thought better of it, and rose to his feet.

"I'll see what I can do," he said and walked from the office.

"Reckon we can trust him?" Dusty asked.

"No," smiled Lucienne. "But he daren't doublecross us after what I told him. Especially as I let him know how I left letters behind to be passed out if anything happens to us."

Ten minutes later Cornwall returned to the office. He brought in a middle-sized man of indeterminate age and who dressed like a respectable craftsman.

"This's Saul Paupin—," Cornwall began, then found his introduction unnecessary.

"Annie!" Paupin gasped, advancing with his right hand held out. "Annie Buckhalter. I heard that you were dead."

"So did a lot of folks," smiled Lucienne and turned to Cornwall. "You've done good, real good, Harwold."

"Then how about doing your part?" Cornwall asked. "They're getting restless out there."

Clearly Lucienne regarded the man as entirely satisfactory for she asked only if he would help her by opening a safe and he agreed eagerly. Telling Dusty to stay with Paupin, Lucienne followed Belle and Cornwall from the room. Paupin asked no questions about the proposed robbery during the few minutes before Cornwall returned and asked if they wanted to see the fight.

"I'll put you at a table by the office here," he offered. "If you want anything to drink—"

"A glass of beer'll do me," Dusty replied and Paupin requested the same.

Maybe Cornwall hoped to pump Dusty about the robbery, but the chance did not present itself. Even as he seated Dusty and Paupin, a waiter came up with word that the main guests of the evening requested their host's company.

Suddenly a hush fell on the room, then a low rumble of excitement rippled through the crowd. Three women crossed from a side room and climbed up to enter the ring. Clad in dresses, two of the trio carried a bucket, bottle of water, towel and the other gear prize-fight seconds used.

Not that Dusty paid much attention to the pair, being more interested in the third woman. She would be two inches shorter than Belle, although out-weighing the Rebel Spy by several pounds. Medium long blonde hair, gathered in a bunch on either side of the head, framed a sullen yet good-looking face. Standing in her corner, the blonde looked even more blocky than Ruby Toot, yet had hard flesh not flabby fat. Clad in a sleeveless bodice, which showed plainly she wore nothing beneath it, and black tights, the woman gave an impression of strength and power.

"I hope your gal knows what she's doing," Paupin remarked. "English Flo's near on as good as any man I've ever seen."

So was Belle, Dusty mused, but in a different style of fighting. Dusty knew little about prize-fighting, but doubted whether her knowledge of *savate*, or the *karate* and *ju-jitsu* moves he taught her during the sea voyage to and from Matamoros, would be of use, as they might contravene the rules.

In the ring, the referee announced to a suddenly silent crowd that Ruby Toot had met with an injury. Disappointed and angry murmurs rose and he hurriedly assured his audience that a substitute had been found. Although some of the crowd began to complain, they fell silent when Belle made her appearance. Accompanied by Lucienne and one of Ruby Toot's seconds, Belle walked to the ring and climbed in.

True to his word, Cornwall rigged the girl with a ring costume. Dressed in the same manner as English Flo, with the garments fitting just as snugly, Belle's appearance more than compensated the women-hungry male crowd for Ruby's absence.

Possibly the worst part of the ordeal for Belle was facing the crowd in such scanty attire. Not even her male clothing was so revealing as the borrowed outfit and she rarely wore the shirt and breeches when in general company. However the thought of her mission's importance drove down her objections and she forced herself to ignore the comments of the crowd. To take her mind off the audience, she studied English Flo. Although the blonde had the advantage of weight and possibly strength, Belle doubted whether she would be fast-moving. Speed then would be the weapon Belle must use, relying on her superb physical condition to out-last her more experienced opponent.

The preliminaries went by fast, with the referee warning the girls that biting, gouging, scratching and jumping on an opponent who was down would not be tolerated. Going back to her corner, Belle turned and waited for what seemed a long time until the bout commenced.

"Time!" ordered the timekeeper, seated outside the ring.

Rounds as such did not exist, each lasting as long as both girls kept their feet. When one went down, the round ended and she must toe the line ready to fight on after sixty seconds or lose the bout. The timekeeper's function was to check on the period between a knock-down and toeing the line.

Flo studied Belle with interest as they approached each other and figured the slim girl knew enough about fist-fighting to be dangerous. For her part, Belle watched Flo adopt the typical style of the male pugilist. While bare-fist pugilists of the day tended to stand up and slug, the lightly-

built Creoles of New Orleans already used foot-work which,
along with dodging and weaving, would oust the old style
fighters eventually. Having learned her lessons well, Belle
used the *savate* stance. She kept her elbows into her sides
and pointing downwards, right arm in front and its fist just
below eye level, left just above the height of the solar plexus.
Although *savate's* main emphasis centred on kicking, the
fists were also used; so the stance she adopted offered good
offensive and defensive possibilities.

Before the blonde came within punching distance, Belle
made use of her longer reach. Three times in rapid succes-
sion Belle's raised right fist stabbed out to smack into Flo's
face. Even at the end of their flight, the punches stung
enough to halt the blonde's advance. Rocking back a step,
Flo shook her head and thrust forward determinedly. In
doing so, she left herself open for a body kick and Belle
prepared to launch it. Then Belle hesitated. While no mention of kicking had been made by the referee, she felt sure
it would be against the rules.

While hesitating, Belle learned that Flo could move with
deceptive speed. Taking her chance, the blonde lunged forward and crashed a solid right into Belle's ribs. Belle gasped,
for the blow had not been light, and danced back just too
late to avoid Flo's follow-up punch to the side of her jaw.
As Belle staggered, Flo bored in and flung punches with
both fists at the slender body. Pain and anger caused Belle
to hit back and the girls exchanged punches in the centre
of the ring.

That proved the wrong way for Belle, being out-weighed
by the stocky blonde, although it took almost thirty seconds
for the idea to sink home. Dancing clear, Belle avoided a
hook aimed at her bust and ripped a hard right to Flo's cheek
before going out of range.

Following her decision, Belle danced around the blonde
and tossed long-range punches over the other's guard. Although the blows reached her opponent, Belle could not
land them at full power. However they stung the blonde and

Belle hoped to goad the other into some rash move. The hope did not materialise. Despite using the same tactics as male pugilists of the day, Flo clearly used her brains and did not rely on brute force. She quickly realised Belle's intention and countered it by doggedly ignoring the stinging fists while trying to crowd the other girl into a ring corner.

For almost three minutes Belle managed to avoid being trapped or taking more than the occasional punch. She landed a few hard blows in return and her stinging knuckles homed often enough to leave a reddened patch under Flo's left eye and to start the blonde's nose trickling blood. Each time Belle found herself at close range it came about through her preparing to kick and calling off the move at the last moment.

After sinking a hard left into Flo's chest, Belle again began to wind up for a kick and held it back. She felt Flo's left fist rip into her stomach, croaked and began to double over. Across whipped the blonde's right, colliding with the side of Belle's head before she had time to recover from the left. Down went Belle, sprawling on to the canvas-covered wooden floor. Dazed, winded and hurt, Belle tried to rise. She felt hands take hold of her arms and lift her erect. Supported by Lucienne and the borrowed second, she was returned to her corner and seated on a stool while receiving treatment.

"That kid's good," Paupin remarked to Dusty.

The small Texan did not reply, but his concern grew as he watched Belle rise for the start of the second round. Knowing her, he doubted if she would follow the safe course of avoiding as much punishment as possible while giving the crowd a reasonable show, then fail to toe the line after the end of a round. Unless he missed his guess, she intended to carry the affair through to its conclusion.

So it seemed as Belle began to fight the second round. Some of the crowd had not seen girls fighting in a ring before and came along expecting nothing more than a good laugh. The derision they might have felt rapidly died away as Flo and Belle put on a bout every bit as tough as could any two men.

Belle lost the second round, going down after a dogged pursuit found her trapped against the ropes. In addition to being able to hit hard, Flo could take punishment; and she needed to, for not all Belle's punches landed at the end of their flight. Yet when she did get within range, Flo handed back as much, if not more than she received.

More than that, Flo knew the game far better than Belle. In the third round, having taken a punch in the right eye which partially blinded her, Flo was wide open and Belle went in to make the most of the chance. Sinking a wicked left into Flo's bust, the girl drew a moan of agony and sent the blonde stumbling away. Before Belle could do more, Flo slipped to one knee and ended the round. Nor did Flo give Belle a chance to capitalize on the advantage. At the first hint of trouble in the fourth round, the blonde cut her losses and sank down again.

By the time the fifth round started Flo had thrown off the effects. She took Belle by surprise, moving straight in and making a two-handed attack. With punches raining on her body, or jabbing into her face, Belle could not use her footwork or speed. So she hit back, throwing both hands as fast and hard as she could. Cheers and yells of encouragement rose from the crowd as the girls slugged it out toe to toe, drowning Lucienne's yelled advice. So Belle did not hear her friend telling her to go down and end the round. Instead she took a beating.

So did Flo. Closing, she locked her arms around Belle's body and began to squeeze. Belle croaked, feeling as if her rib cage would be crushed at any moment. Yet the referee made no attempt to separate them. Placing her head under Belle's chin, Flo forced upwards, holding herself so close that the other girl could not use her fists. On other occasions when Flo used that devastating bear-hug, her opponent forgot fist-fighting and grabbed that conveniently fastened hair;

to waste valuable energy on something which hurt but did little damage.

Only this time she fought a girl skilled in more than one form of self-defence. Remembering a trick Dusty taught her, Belle pressed her thumbs into the sensitive mastoid area under the ears and at the hinge of the jawbones. Although the pain did not incapacitate Flo, it caused her to loosen her hold. With a thrust of her hard body, Flo bellied Belle backwards. Winded, exhausted and body throbbing in pain, Belle doubled over and fell against the ropes. To her amazement, she saw Flo's foot driving up to catch her in the body. Gagging with nausea, Belle collapsed to the floor.

Half a minute's seconding was needed before Belle recovered enough to be able to understand what Lucienne said to her. Lying back on the stool, her body a mass of pain, nose bloody, left eye swollen and discoloured, Belle looked up at her friend and the words began to take effect.

"Give it up, Belle," Lucienne said. "You've done enough."

"Sh—She kicked me!" Belle gasped, indignation preventing her from taking the advice.

"She's allowed to, and use any standing wrestling holds," the second put in. "Hell, didn't you know that?"

"No!" Belle admitted. "But I do now."

Flo did not expect Belle to come out and toe the line. Even seeing the slim girl approach the ring centre, she doubted if there would be any trouble in ending the fight that round. So she advanced confidently, yet watchful and alert.

So far Belle had only used her fists, giving no sign of either kicking or using any of the standing wrestling holds permitted by the rules. She aimed to change all that. With only the tights covering her feet, she realised kicking with the toe would hurt her more than Flo, but she had other methods at her disposal. Rotating half a turn to the left before Flo reached punching range, Belle tilted her body over from the waist. She drew her right leg up and shot it outwards. Rising up, the bottom of her heel drove into the point of Flo's jaw with considerable force. Back snapped the blonde head as Flo halted in her tracks, dazed and momentarily helpless. Nor did Belle give her time to recover. Bringing down her leg from the horizontal high kick, Belle used it as a pivot to turn and snap a wicked stamping kick full into the pit of the blonde's stomach. Although the blonde had taken hard punches down there without any undue distress, the force of the kick doubled her over like a closing jack-knife.

Jumping in close, Belle sent her left knee crashing full into the centre of the blonde's face. Its force pulped the nose to bloody ruin and lifted Flo erect. Just as when she dealt with the fake preacher in Arkansas, Belle finished the attack with a vicious right cross that exploded her fist against Flo's jaw and sent the woman sprawling head first into one of the ring posts.

A minute dragged by, with Flo's seconds doing all they could to revive her. Although they worked hard, she still lay limp and helpless in her corner when time was called.

"I—I've won!" Belle gasped to Lucienne.

"You won," she agreed. "Now let's get out of here as quick as we can."

CHAPTER TWELVE

A Mighty Persuasive Young Man

Although the officers at Cornwall's table expressed a desire to entertain Belle in honour of her victory, Lucienne insisted that the girl's injuries must be treated first. Avoiding all other attempts to delay them, the woman hustled Belle across the room. Dusty and Paupin rose, following the women into Cornwall's office where Lucienne sent the second to collect some of the gear deliberately forgotten on helping Belle from the ring.

"How'd you feel, Belle?" Dusty asked as the girl sank exhaustedly into a chair at the desk and Lucienne closed the door behind the second.

"Not good," Belle admitted and winced as she touched her ribs. "I don't think anything's broken, though."

"Get your blouse and skirt on, Belle!" ordered Lucienne, bolting the door. Then she gathered the remainder of the girl's property from where it lay on the desk and went on, "I want to get out of here."

"Belle needs time to get over that fight," Dusty objected.

"Only we don't have time to let her," Lucienne pointed out. "Look, Dusty, Cornwall can't just pull out and leave those officers. I want to get clear before he can."

"How do we get out, Annie?" Paupin asked.

"Through that door there," Lucienne answered, indicating the room's second exit. "It leads into the side-alley. Reckon you can unlock it?"

"I've yet to see the lock I can't open," Paupin stated calmly.

Watching the man cross the room and bend to examine the lock, Lucienne grinned and said, "I bet Cornwall didn't know Saul and I're good friends. He'd've tried to get somebody else if he had known."

Working slowly, for each move cost her plenty in pain to her aching, bruised body, Belle drew on her blouse, shirt and shoes over the borrowed bodice and tights. By the time she had dressed, Paupin straightened from the lock and pulled the door open. Dressed, Belle looked passable. The second had managed to stop her nose and mouth bleeding during the rests between the final two rounds, so only the girl's enlarged upper lip and swollen eye gave visible signs of the fight. That would not be noticeable once on the streets, although Belle could not move at any speed.

With Belle's parasol in one hand and underclothing tucked under her arm, Lucienne stepped cautiously into the alley separating the Green Peacock from the neighbouring building. Dusty and Paupin took the girl's arms and helped her along as Lucienne led them to the rear of the building.

"Where'd you keep your tools, Saul?" she asked. "We'll collect them and you can spend the night with us."

"It'd be best," he admitted. "Watch we're not followed, Annie. I've a room not far from here."

Taking Paupin's advice, Lucienne kept a careful watch as the safe-breaker led them to his home. She saw nothing to disturb her and felt certain that leaving so soon after the fight took Cornwall by surprise. At last Paupin halted and indicated a small rooming house as his home. Telling the others to wait, he entered the building.

"Reckon you can trust him, Lucienne?" asked Dusty.

"Like I trust Jim Bludso, or you two," she answered. "Enough to take him back to the Busted Boiler with us and tell him the truth."

"Is that wise?" Belle inquired, leaning against Dusty's arm.

"Saul lost his brother and son fighting the Yankees. He's no love for them."

The subject lapsed, for both Belle and Dusty knew they could rely on Lucienne's judgement. Soon after, Paupin came from the house and joined them with a leather bag in his hand.

"Have you everything you'll need, Saul?" Lucienne said.

"Sure," he replied. "Let's go." Then as he turned, a change came over him. "Keep walking and talking," he ordered.

With the bag in his hand Paupin could not help Belle, and Lucienne took his place. At first he strolled along with them, but dropped back as soon as they turned a corner. Flattening himself against the wall, he peeped cautiously around in the direction from which they came. Satisfied that his early view had been correct, Paupin followed and caught up to the others.

"Cornwall's smarter than you figured, Annie," he declared. "When I came out of the house, I caught a glimpse of Slippery Sid watching me from up the street."

"I should've figured on it," the woman answered. "Cornwall would know we'd come here to collect your tools. We'll have to stop Slippery following us."

"Happen we can find the right sort of place," Dusty drawled. "I'll see if I can persuade him to leave us be."

"You'd best not start shooting, Dusty," Lucienne warned.

"Don't figure to," Dusty replied.

"Slippery's not the biggest, nor toughest jasper Cornwall hires," Paupin put in, "but he's good with a razor and he's got Latour to back him up. They're a rough handful."

"I'll mind it," promised Dusty. "Let's find the right kind of place."

"Tell us what you want and we'll try to find it for you," Belle stated, having the advantage of knowing Dusty's ability in the art of bare-handed defence.

The two men following Dusty's party knew their work and kept well back in their attempts at avoiding being seen. Much to their annoyance, Slippery and Latour noticed their victims turn off into almost deserted streets which did not make for easy dogging. However the emptiness worked two ways in that they could hear the other party ahead of them even when out of sight. When the opportunity presented itself, the two men moved into visual range. They saw Lucienne and Paupin on either side of the girl, with Dusty walking ahead and carrying the safebreaker's bag. After winding about for a time, the quartet turned a corner and disappeared from sight. Realising that the others had entered an alley and might be lost, Slippery increased his pace and Latour followed obediently. Turning the corner, both men saw the bulk of the party ahead of them.

Standing flattened against the wall just around the corner, Dusty watched his friends walk away and listened to the sound of approaching feet. With Belle so exhausted, there would be no chance of losing the following men any other way. So he prepared to make his move.

Sometimes the subject of spies had come up for discussion in the Regiment's mess, with many a comment on the easy life such people must lead being passed among the younger officers. Dusty now realised just how wrong they had been. None of his friends back at the Regiment even started to think of the numerous details a spy needed, at his, or her fingertips. Nor would any of them have guessed at the kind of things that could go wrong on a spy's assignment. Not the least being that the spies had aroused the avarice and interest of a dangerous criminal. It fell on Dusty to remove the menace from their tracks.

One thing Dusty knew for sure, he could not act in a

sporting manner when dealing with the two men. Too much
hung in the balance for him to give Slippery Sid and Latour
an even break. So he waited, tense and ready, as the men
turned the corner. Slippery Sid stood six foot, with a lean,
gaunt frame, while Latour was a couple of inches smaller
and stocky. Which meant both of them possessed a considerable height-weight advantage over the small Texan. However Dusty had surprise on his side.

Lunging forward, Dusty heard a startled expression break
from Latour, and struck at Slippery Sid. While most Occidental men of the period would have crashed a fist into
Slippery's jaw, Dusty knew a far more effective way of
handling him. The small Texan struck with a clenched fist,
but not in the accepted manner. Instead he used the *hito-
sashiyubi-ipponken*, the forefinger-fist, with the forefinger's
knuckle projecting beyond the others. Such a blow could
be directed against the solar-plexus, or the *jinchu* collection
of nerve centres in the centre of the top lip, with devastating
effect; but Dusty aimed for neither. His hand struck home
under Slippery's chin, smashing into his prominent adam's
apple. In striking, Dusty tried to land his blow hard enough
to create a temporary paralysis and unconsciousness, but
not so as to seriously injure or kill the man. A croak of
agony broke from Slippery and he stumbled backwards,
feeling as if somebody had thrust an iron knob into his
throat.

Already Latour began to turn and face Dusty, right hand
fanning to his pocket. Having thought ahead, Dusty did not
need to plan further action. From striking Slippery, he
whipped straight into a *mae keri* forward kick that slammed
his boot full into the pit of Latour's stomach. Letting out a
winded screech, Latour doubled over. His hands clawed at
his middle though he still retained enough control over himself to stagger forward in an attempt to avoid a knee to the
face. Although Dusty had hoped to end the matter with his
knee, he wasted no time in trying to move to a position
where he could. Bending his right arm, he swung it up and

down. His elbow struck home right where it would do most good, at the base of the skull, and Latour went down like a back-broken rabbit.

Only just in time Dusty heard the sound of Slippery's muffled gasping draw nearer. In his desire not to strike too hard, Dusty had erred the other way. While feeling half-strangled, the thin man was still on his feet and, if anything, even more dangerous than before. Around lashed the open cutthroat razor in Slippery's hand in a wicked downwards slash. The steel missed, but by a very slender margin, to be whipped back upwards again. Such a blow had succeeded on other occasions when the first slash missed and the victim tried to close with Slippery. It might have again, for Dusty had begun to move forward. Seeing his danger, Dusty thrust himself rearwards and once more avoided the murderous blade.

Up went the razor and Dusty moved as if to try to block it. Having witnessed the small Texan's speed, Slippery hurried his roundhouse cut just as Dusty hoped. Checking his forward motion, Dusty swayed his torso out of the radius of the razor's swing. Unable to stop himself, Slippery bent over and the razor pointed towards the ground away from Dusty. Even as the man prepared to cut up again, Dusty pivoted into a stamping kick which thudded home against the other's rib cage. Slippery cried out in pain as two ribs broke and the force of the kick propelled him into the wall of the nearer building. Leaping over the razor, which had fallen from its owner's hand when the kick landed, Dusty drove a *tegatana* chop with the edge of his hand against the back of the man's neck. Down went Slippery and Dusty heard a footstep behind him. Whipping around, he prepared to deal with whoever made it.

"Dusty!" gasped Lucienne's voice urgently. "It's me. Are you all right?"

"I reckon so," he replied. "This pair won't be following anybody for a spell though."

A match rasped and in its glow Lucienne studied the two

sprawled out shapes on the ground.

"You're right about that," she breathed and awe as much as a need for secrecy kept her voice down. "I don't know how you do it, but you're a mighty persuasive young man. Come on, Belle insisted that one of us come back to see how you made out. Let's show her you're all right."

"Reckon there's any chance of Cornwall finding us now?" Dusty inquired as they walked along the alley.

"I doubt it. He'll maybe try, though."

"To help the Yankees?"

"To cut himself into a share of the loot. Only he'll have to find us first."

Whatever action Cornwall might decide to take, he would need to locate Dusty's party first. Clearly he regarded the two as ample to trail them to their hideout, for Lucienne and Paupin kept a careful watch without seeing any sign of more of the saloonkeeper's men. Paupin appeared surprised at being taken to the Busted Boiler and remarked that it would be the last place Cornwall thought of looking for them. Letting them in by a rear door, Lucienne led the way upstairs to the room which had been prepared as her hideout.

Not until seated in the room, behind drawn curtains and a locked door did Paupin learn the truth about the safe he would be asked to break open. He hesitated only for one minute, then nodded his agreement.

"I'm still on," he stated.

"There'll be five hundred dollars in Yankee gold for you after you've done it," Belle promised.

"I'd do it for nothing, young lady. It's for the South."

"How about when it's done?" asked Dusty. "What'll Cornwall do?"

"What can he do?" Belle countered. "He'll know what's happened, but he can hardly say anything."

"I'll make sure of *that*," Lucienne promised firmly. "Tomorrow morning I'll send him a warning that if he tries another trick like with Slippery, I'll let the Yankees hear what I know. And after the job's over, I'll let him know that if he talks I'll fix it so the Yankees hear he planned the whole thing."

"Will he believe you?"

"He'll be too cautious not to, Dusty," Belle guessed. "Especially as he's managed to keep his place going and bringing in money. I'd say he'd not chance spoiling it."

As his companions appeared satisfied that Cornwall did not pose a serious threat, Dusty relaxed. Soon after, Jim Bludso returned. Seeing Belle's facial damage, he forgot to give the news that his part of the affair was well in hand.

"What the hell happened to you?" he growled.

"I met another of your 'sisters,'" Belle answered coldly. "Sister Ruby."

"Ruby Toot?" Jim said. "I'd forgotten about her. I'm sorry about that, Miss Boyd. See, she was going with a Yankee Army engineer working on the new defences they set up. I got to know her and picked up details of the work they did. Trouble being the engineer left soon after and Ruby figured I should take his place."

"What if Cornwall sends somebody around here asking questions?" Dusty put in. "He'll likely learn what caused the fuss between Belle and that Toot gal."

"He won't learn a thing," Jim replied. "Early tomorrow I'll see those Yankee brass-pounders and let on that you stayed the night here with me, Miss Boyd."

"You'll ruin my good name," smiled the girl. "But Cornwall may move sooner than that."

"What do we do then?" the engineer asked.

"Play smarter than he does," Belle replied.

At about the same time that Belle laid her plans to circumvent Cornwall's efforts to find her, the man learned of the failure to follow her party to its hideout. He had made excuses to his guests on learning of Belle's departure and contented himself with the knowledge that Slippery Sid and Latour waited at Paupin's home ready to trail them. When the battered pair returned, interrupting an enjoyable evening, Cornwall started to ask questions. First he learned the

cause of the trouble between Belle and Ruby Toot. Talking
with the three petty officers, Cornwall could not decide
whether the girl had been one of Jim Bludso's 'sisters' or
merely a victim of mistaken identity. While the most sober
of the petty officers insisted that the 'sister' visiting Bludso
had a been a brunette, as opposed to Annie Buckhalter's
girl having blonde hair, Cornwall decided to check. Calling
over one of his most reliable men, Cornwall gave orders.

"Yeah?" Jim Bludso called sleepily in answer to a knocking
at his room's outside door. "What's up?"

"Got a message for you, Mr. Bludso," a male voice
answered.

"Can't it wait until morning?"

"No, sir."

Outside Jim's door, the man saw a lamp lit and its glow
drew closer. From all the signs, Jim had just left his bed.
Naked to the waist and supporting his pants with one hand,
bare-foot and with hair rumpled untidily, the big engineer
scowled at his visitor in the light of the small lamp.

"Who-all is it, Jim honey?" asked a girl's voice from
inside the room.

"Hush your mouth, gal!" Jim barked.

By moving around in a casual manner, the visitor found
he could make out the bed. A shape moved uneasily in it
and, although unable to see much, he judged it to be the
female speaker. Further than that, a mass of brunette hair
showed in contrast to the pillow.

As if noticing the man's interest, Jim reached out a hand
to draw the door shut and hide his 'bed-mate' from view.
Then he growled out a demand for information as to the
reason for the visit.

"There's Yankee ironsides due in early tomorrow and
they want you to gather a gang ready to help clean its
engines," the man answered.

Although he received a blistering cursing for disturbing
Jim with such unimportant news, the man went away contented. Returning to the Green Peacock, he told Cornwall

that the brunette was still with Jim Bludso. Cornwall decided
that the Yankee petty officer either made a mistake, or
deliberately stirred up trouble with Ruby Toot in the hope
of seeing a fight before the one arranged in the ring. While
disinterested in Ruby's injury, Cornwall cursed bitterly, his
invective being directed at the time wasted in checking the
story. There would be little or no chance of finding where
the safe was that "Annie Buckhalter" planned to rob in time
to grab off a portion of the loot, if she intended to strike
that night. Maybe it would be for the best. He would not
be too sorry to learn that the woman brought off her proposed
robbery and slipped safely out of New Orleans; "Annie
Buckhalter" knew far too much about him for comfort.

Jim Bludso put out the lamp when the man reached the
foot of the stairs, but did not return to his bed. Instead he
stood by the window and watched his visitor depart, while
drawing on his shirt.

"I reckon he fell for it, Miss Boyd. Shall I follow him?"

The bed creaked as Belle swung her bare feet out of it.
Dressed in her male clothing, less the riding boots, she
crossed the room and halted at Bludso's side.

"I'd say let him go and tell his boss," she replied. "He's
certain that you have a girl in here and I'm sure Cornwall
will think the Yankee brass-pounder made a mistake."

"I'm not sorry that jasper came," Bludso stated. "If he'd
held off much longer, I'd've been asleep."

"I *was*," put in Dusty Fog's voice from the side of the
room.

"And me," Paupin went on. "That's a smart scheme you
thought up, Miss Boyd, but now let's grab some sleep shall
we?"

"Go ahead," smiled the girl, crossing to the interior door
and opening it. "I doubt if they'll try again, so I'm going
to bed. Good night."

With that, the girl left Bludso's room and went to the
one she would share with Lucienne. All in all Belle felt that
the boredom of waiting in the dark for a visit from Corn-

wall's man had been worth while. She felt sure that the saloonkeeper would be fooled and thrown off their trail. That only left the main problem, the destruction of the counterfeiting plant, for them to worry about. Nothing could be done about that until they learned more about the Gaton house's defences. She wondered if the men she met at Lucienne's shop had recovered and made a guess at her mission or identity.

So far neither had. In a room at the military hospital Kaddam lay unconscious and with a fractured skull, while Turnpike waited for the drugs prescribed by the doctor to overcome the pain of his throbbing head and let him sleep. Before he could think of the events at Madam Lucienne's shop, sleep claimed him and he did not wake up until late the following morning.

Even then Turnpike did not rush to resume his interrupted work. Lethargy induced by the drugs kept him content to lie in bed until a recurring thought nagged its way through to him. Had there been more to the affair at the shop than a mere attempt at robbery? Before being sedated, he had learned all he could about the couple's actions and escape; but the doctor insisted that he must sleep before doing anything about it.

Sitting up, Turnpike called for his clothes. For all that, it was late in the afternoon before he entered Lucienne's shop. Making a thorough examination, he found the till empty and the ledger gone. His own people had searched the shop without finding anything to lead them to its owner, or tell of her activities. Yet he felt sure that his information as to her being a Confederate spy was true.

Could the theft of the ledger be more than coincidence? Did Lucienne send those two with orders to collect it and prevent whatever it contained falling into the wrong hands?

Certainly such skill with a gun as the small man showed could not be found in the normal sneak-thief. Turnpike would never forget the speed with which the man drew and fired at him.

Leaving the shop, Turnpike returned to his department's office and read through records, trying to find some report of the small man. Night came with him no nearer to an answer. He sat alone in the office, thinking about the small man. Then he turned his attention to the woman, remembering that she did all the talking and showed a fair turn of speed in handling Kaddam.

Going into the shop, knowing it to be in Yankee hands, called for a special brand of courage. One name leapt instantly to mind in connection with such an act. Belle Boyd, the Rebel Spy, had the audacity and nerve to do it. Yet she was reported to be in Arkansas. It seemed highly unlikely that Lucienne could have contacted Belle Boyd so quickly. Of course the Rebel Spy might have come to New Orleans on some other mission. Turnpike could think of only one thing in New Orleans big enough to attract Belle Boyd. Rising, he dashed from the office in search of a carriage.

CHAPTER THIRTEEN

The Raid

"Six men?" Dusty Fog said in surprise, looking at the big, powerful Negro at Jim Bludso's side.

"That's all," replied Willie, Bludso's striker. "They turns out all the coloured folks afore dark."

"Maybe they move a guard in after dark," Dusty remarked.

"No, sir," Willie answered. "Once in a while they has visitors, but only one or two of 'em at a time. I asked around among the house staff and they know."

"It's possible that they think they don't need a big guard, Dusty," Belle pointed out. "They don't know that we stopped the consignment and hope to avoid attention by not having the house heavily guarded."

"They sure ain't like that Yankee colonel along the street from 'em," Willie commented. "He's done got thirty men on hand all the time guarding him."

"That's a mighty big guard for a colonel's residence, even in occupied territory," Dusty stated. "It's near on half a company."

"There's not been sufficient civic unrest to warrant that big a guard," Belle agreed. "How close to the Gaton house are they, Willie?"

"A quarter of a mile, ma'am," the Negro replied. "Only they'd not need to shout for help. There's a telegraph wire running down the back from Gaton's house to where the colonel lives."

It was mid-afternoon and Dusty's party gathered in Jim Bludso's room to hear Willie give his report. Clearly the big Negro possessed excellent methods of gathering information, for he gave a very clear picture of the house. In far less time than Dusty would have believed possible, Willie had gathered enough details to make planning the raid feasible.

No white man could have done it in so short a time. Posing as a freed, but unemployed slave, Willie visited the Gaton house's servants' entrance and asked for work. Being big, strong, jovial and attractive to women, he ingratiated himself rapidly among the household staff. While it turned out that they could not hope to gain permanent employment for him, the staff let him stay with them. In return for helping with their work, they gave him much information and permitted him to see around both building and grounds. He noticed that the gardens appeared in need of attention, but his offer to do some tidying up met with refusal. For some reason or other, Massa Gaton gave orders that none of the staff must stray from the paths and had discharged one man who started to go amongst the bushes. Although unable to make a search of the garden and learn the reason for the ban, Willie managed to see the telegraph wires.

"They runs across the garden from a downstairs window," he said. "And the one to the colonel's house ain't on its own."

"There're more of them?" asked Dusty.

"Sure are, Cap'n. I saw two more. Only they was fastened about eighteen inches above the ground and to the bushes. Couldn't see where they went and didn't find a chance to look closer."

"You know what they are, Dusty?" Belle put in, the words a statement rather than a question.

"Trip wires," he replied. "The Yankees used them and ground torpedoes up around Little Rock. One end of the wire's fastened to a pull-primer and when you hit it, the charge goes up."

"That's what I thought," the girl confirmed. "Maybe they'll have the torpedoes in place too."

"Give them their due, those Yankees are smart," Dusty said. "Just six men at the house, but a good-sized guard on hand. Not in the house to draw attention and start our folks wondering why they're there, but close enough to arrive in a hurry if they're needed."

"The telegraph manned day and night, most likely," Belle went on.

"You can count on that, ma'am," Willie remarked. "Least-wise there's one room downstairs that's allus got a man in it. Maid I asked allowed he'd got him some scientifical instrument in there, but she didn't know what it was. Way she described it, I'd say it was a telegraph key like I saw a few times on the river."

"Which room, Willie?"

"First on the right at the foot of the main stairs, Cap'n. Door was shut all the time I was there."

"Locked?"

"If it was, the gal didn't mention it."

"I never did like them too easy," Belle sighed. "If we set off whatever's at the end of one of those trip-wires the telegraph operator starts sending a warning, even if the soldiers don't see and hear the explosion."

"Or goes to tapping his key should anybody slip through the wires and get into the house," Dusty continued.

"Can we break in?" Bludso demanded.

"We're going to make a try," Dusty assured him. "We'll

have to go tonight, too if we can."

"The longer we wait, the better chance for Cornwall to find us," Lucienne put in. "Or for the Yankees to hear something and get suspicious. I'd say tonight, if it can be done."

"Are you set, Jim?" Dusty wanted to know.

"Got all we need, Cap'n. We cut open some incendiary shells and poured the stuff into small barrels. A couple of them ought to do all we need. How many men do you want?"

"A few as we can manage with. You, Willy, Saul and—"

"And me," interrupted Belle. "No arguments, Dusty. This's my assignment and I mean to see it through."

"Belle and me then," Dusty finished and grinned at the man. "Giving in to her straight off saves time. She sure is a strong-willed gal.

"Will that be enough?" asked Lucienne. "You don't need more men?"

"It ought to be enough," Dusty answered. "We have to go quietly, so the smaller the party, the better."

"How about you, Lucy gal," Bludso grinned. "You want to come along?"

"Not me," the woman laughed. "The days when I went in for that kind of stuff are long over. I'll stay here ready to do anything that needs doing. How do you intend to play it, Dusty?"

"This's how I reckon," he replied and outlined his plans.

Night found the party Dusty named standing before the Gaton house. With Jim Bludso and Willie as their guides, they passed unnoticed through the town and that despite the kegs and other equipment they carried. For the most part they went by back streets and other deserted ways, but occasionally needed to pass other people. At such time the men gathered around Belle, who was definitely feminine despite her male attire, and gave an impression of being a group of revellers on their way home from some celebration.

Luck favoured them in that they found St. Charles Avenue deserted. The big gates of Gaton's house were closed and locked.

"We'll have to go over the wall," Belle breathed.

"Around the side then," Dusty replied and led the way.

Even in the alley separating Gaton's home from its neighbour, the surrounding wall rose ten feet high and carried pieces of broken glass fixed to its top. When Dusty heard of the added protection, he laid plans to circumvent it. Unfastening the thick roll of blankets he wore slung across his shoulders, Dusty looked to make sure Belle kept watch and then walked to the base of the wall. Already Jim Bludso and Willie had set down the small kegs they carried and stood waiting to do their parts. Placing his right foot into Bludso's cupped hands, Dusty thrust himself upwards with the left. At the same moment Bludso began to lift and Dusty rose up the wall. Willie's hands went under Dusty's left foot and the two big men hoisted the small Texan into the air until he was level with the top of the wall, then held him there.

Supported by the two men, Dusty spread a thick pad of blanket over the top of the wall. Although the broken edges of the glass made uncomfortable bumps, they could not cut through several thicknesses of the folded material. Sitting astride the padding, Dusty gave the grounds a quick scrutiny and saw no sign of guards. Already Paupin was being hoisted up by the two men and at Dusty's signal took a seat facing him. Leaving her post, Belle joined the men. She unslung the coil of rope from her shoulder and tossed one end to Dusty so he could haul up Paupin's tool bag. Next Belle came up and joined the two men on top of the wall.

"I'll go down first," she whispered.

Gripping the rope, Belle slid down it to the ground with Dusty holding the other end. The girl kept close to the wall, taking the bag which Paupin lowered and then the two kegs. On the other side of the wall, Willie handed Bludso up to the waiting men and then received their help to climb up and drop down, joining Belle.

"Keep close to the wall!" Dusty ordered.

When making his plans, Dusty gambled on there being no trip-wires or ground torpedoes close to the surrounding walls, or on the main path to the house. Unless he missed his guess, the Yankees would expect an attacking party to approach through the cover of the bushes and must have laid their defences accordingly. So he planned to reach the house by the front path; doing the unexpected often paid dividends.

"I'd like to unlock that gate before going to the house, Cap'n," Paupin breathed. "If we have to run for it, there won't be time."

"It's your game we're playing, Saul," Dusty answered. "Go to it."

By the time they reached the gates, Dusty knew the first part of his gamble had been successful. They had encountered no trip-wires or ground torpedoes so close to the wall. Nor had Paupin found any difficulty in opening the heavy lock securing the gates. Before going further, the party took precautions against being recognised. Each one carried a cloth hood, made up that evening, designed to cover the head and trail down to the shoulders. In addition the men wore clothes which could not lead to their being identified. Slipping on their hoods, taking care that they could see through the eye-holes, the party advanced silently along the edge of the path.

Lights glowed in the main hall and a few other rooms, showing that at least some of the six men were present and not yet in bed. The sight did not cause any thought among the party that Dusty's plans were going wrong. Working on the assumption that the Yankees would expect any such an attempt to come between midnight and dawn, Dusty arranged for them to reach the house just after nine o'clock. In that way, he hoped to take the defenders by surprise.

Not that Dusty intended to rush the front door. Close to the house, he left the path and walked along the side of the building. According to Willie, the servants could walk around the outside of the house provided they stuck close to the wall. So Dusty took a chance that there would be no protective devices in that area. He hoped that the Yankees did not go to the trouble of rigging trip-wires or ground torpedoes each night and removing them before the staff arrived in the morning. For all that Dusty walked along with extreme care, feeling at the ground ahead delicately before chancing his weight on it.

At last they reached the rear of the house and found it, as Dusty hoped, silent without signs of occupation. Moving by the small Texan, Paupin took the lead. He had already decided that tackling the kitchen door would be a waste of time as it was bolted in addition to the lock. So he examined one of the windows and nodded in satisfaction. Opening the tool bag, Paupin took out a can of molasses and a sheet of thick paper. After smearing some of the molasses on one side of the paper, he applied its adhesive surface to the pane of glass separating him from the window catch. Next he drew a glazier's glass-cutter from his bag and carefully ran its working edge around the sides of the pane. Dropping the cutter into his jacket pocket, he took hold of the edge of the paper with one hand and tapped its centre with the other. A faint click sounded and the pane moved inwards a trifle. With a firm but gentle pull, Paupin drew the pane, firmly held to the paper, towards him and passed it to Belle.

"I'll go in and unfasten the door," Paupin offered, slipping back the window catch and raising the sash.

Slipping silently through the open window, Paupin disappeared into the building. In a surprisingly short time the kitchen door opened and he grinned at the surprised faces of his companions.

"That was quick," Dusty said.

"The key was in the lock," Paupin admitted. "Everything's quiet enough."

On entering the kitchen Dusty and Belle crossed straight to its inner door. Bludso and Willie set down their kegs while Dusty eased open the door and looked along the dimly-lit passage which led to the front of the building. Followed by Belle, the small Texan crept along the passage. Ahead of them lay a corner and, around it, the main hall. Just as they approached the corner, Belle and Dusty heard footsteps coming towards them.

The man who came around the corner clearly had no suspicion of their presence. Seeing them before him, he came to a halt and stared. Given a chance, he might have made trouble for he had size and weight in addition to a Navy Colt stuck in his waistband. Only he did not receive the opportunity to make use of either his heftiness or the firearm. Up lashed Belle's right foot, driving hard into the pit of the man's groin. Coming so unexpectedly and hard, the kick stopped any outcry the man meant to raise and doubled him over. Dusty followed up Belle's kick with remarkably smooth timing and team-work. Around lashed his left arm in *a tegatana* chop to the back of the man's neck, dropping him silent and unconscious to the floor.

"One!" Belle breathed.

"Hawg-tie him, Jim!" Dusty ordered. "Let's see to some of the others, Belle."

Leaving Bludso and Willie to attend to securing the first prisoner, Dusty and Belle continued to move stealthily along the passage. When making his plans, Dusty decided that Paupin must stay in the background until after the occupants of the house had been secured. They could not replace the safe-breaker if he should be injured, so Dusty refused to take any chances. On reaching the end of the passage, Dusty and Belle looked into the main hall. A wide staircase ran down from the first floor to the centre of the hall. Doors gave access to various rooms off the hall, but only one of them interested Dusty. First item on his agenda was the capture of the telegraph key so that no warning might be passed to the waiting soldiers. From where he and Belle crouched at the side of the stairs, they could see through the open door of the first room on the right. It appeared to be empty; certainly no man sat at the table on which rested the telegraph key.

Voices sounded as a door at the left of the hall opened and footsteps thudded, coming in the direction of the stairs. There would be no time to back off into the passage, nor dare Dusty and Belle chance crouching by the stairs in the hope of not being seen.

Thrusting himself forward, Dusty landed before the men. He went straight into a gun-fighter's crouch and the Army Colt flowed from his waistband. Combined with their surprise at Dusty's sudden, unexpected appearance, his speed on the draw caused the men to freeze. There were four of them, all in their shirt-sleeves and none armed. That left only one to be accounted for, unless Willie had made a mistake in his reckoning.

"Don't make a sound, any of you!" Dusty growled, his gun making a casual arc that seemed to single out each man individually without losing the drop on the remainder. Slowly Dusty and Belle moved forward and he went on, "Back towards the wall real easy and quiet."

Obediently the quartet backed away, keeping spread out just far enough to prevent any one of them taking cover behind the rest. Dusty wanted to get the men in a position where he could make them lean with palms on the wall and bodies inclined so that sudden movement would be impossible. Then tying them up would be easy.

Unnoticed by either Dusty or Belle, a plump, well-dressed man appeared at the head of the stairs. He took in the scene and backed away silently into a room, to emerge a second or two later holding a Navy Colt. Although he lined the gun on Dusty, the man held his fire. At that range he doubted if he could make a hit, and so he began to tiptoe down the stairs. Although Dusty and Belle saw the glances darted behind them by the quartet, each suspected a trick. However the girl started to turn her head, meaning to look and make sure no danger threatened them.

Having finished tying up the first captive, Jim Bludso

came into sight, his knife in his hand. He saw the man on
the stairs. Even without recognising the man as Gaton, the
Confederate printer who sold his skill to the Yankees, Bludso
could not have acted in any other way. Even as one of the
quarted prepared to yell a warning, Bludso threw his knife
so that it passed between the staircase rail in its flight at
Gaton. Steel flickered through the air, sinking into Gaton's
plump throat. He gurgled, jerked and fired the Colt, but its
bullet did no more than shatter a vase by the door. Then,
gagging and choking on his own blood, the traitor crumpled
forward and crashed down the stairs.

Instinctively Belle and Dusty swung their heads in the
direction of the shot. Leaping forward, the biggest man
struck down Dusty's gun arm, gripping it in both his hands
to try to shake the revolver free. A second leaped to lock
his arms around Belle, holding her as he yelled an order.

"Get to the telegraph!"

After throwing his knife, Bludso charged across the hall,
tackling the third man and Willie dashed towards the telegraph room. Swinging around at its door the Negro faced
the approaching fourth member of Gaton's guard and they
disappeared into the room.

Deciding that wearing her gunbelt might attract unwanted
attention, Belle had left it at the Busted Boiler. However
she had the special bracelet on her left wrist. The man
gripped her around the upper arms and from the side, in a
position where she could not kick him hard enough to effect
a release. That did not stop her getting her hands together.
Quickly she eased the bracelet off with her right hand, then
raked its razor-sharp edge across the man's upper wrist.
With a yell of pain he loosened his hold. Even as Belle
drove her left elbow crashing into the man's ribs to send
him stumbling away, she saw Dusty's assailant sail over the
small Texan's shoulder.

Willie came sprawling through the door of the telegraph
room, his hood twisted around so that its eye-holes faced
the rear. Before he could save himself, he crashed to the

floor. Snarling in rage, the fourth man appeared at the door. Then he realised what he must do and put aside thoughts of attacking the Negro. Turning the man started to make for the table again.

Racing across the hall, Belle hurdled over Willie and as she landed bounded into the room again. Her feet smashed into the white man's shoulders, hurling him across the room. On landing from the leaping high kick, Belle flung herself at the table in an attempt to unscrew the wires from the key. While she tried to free the first wire, a hand fell on her shoulder. Swinging around faster than the man pulled, Belle lashed up her right hand to rake the bracelet across his face. Blood spurted and the man fell back a pace in agony. Placing her foot against his stomach, Belle shoved hard. In the hall Willie was just turning his hood so he could see again when the man came backwards through the telegraph-room's door. Still on his knees, the Negro linked hands and smashed them into the back of the man's knees to bring him crashing down.

Crouching ready to attack again, Belle saw Willie leap on to the man and gave her attention to the urgent matter of disabling the telegraph key. Swiftly she disconnected the wires, hurled the key-box against the wall and then darted into the hall ready to help her friends. She found her services would not be needed and the situation under control. Although Bludso knelt holding his side and muttering curses and Dusty had lost his hood but gained a bloody nose, they need not worry for the four guards sprawled all around them.

"Are you all right, Belle?" Dusty asked.

"I'll live," she replied. "How about you?"

"I'm the same as you. Make a start with Saul while we tend to this bunch."

Leaving the men to tie up their groaning, helpless enemies, Belle went to the foot of the stairs. Her face showed distaste as she knelt by Gaton's body and searched its pockets in the hope of finding the safe keys. Failing to do so, she and Paupin went upstairs and made a quick but thorough examination of the man's room. Again they failed to produce the keys.

"It's as I expected," Belle admitted. "He probably hands them to the soldiers after the house staff leave at night. Let's take a look at the safe."

Returning to the hall, Belle and Paupin entered the study as being the most likely place to house the safe. The guess proved correct and Paupin looked over the steel box with faint contempt.

"They're sure easy," he commented. "I could open it with a bobby-pin."

"Do you want one?" Belle smiled.

"Naw! I've brought my tools, so I may as well use them. Go tell the fellers to start getting ready to leave. This won't take long."

CHAPTER FOURTEEN

Miss Boyd Renews an Acquaintance

Although Paupin probably could not have opened the safe with a bobby-pin, he found little difficulty in doing so using his tools. While the safe-breaker handled his part of the affair, all the others worked hard. Half an hour later Belle Boyd stood watching the counterfeiting plates, faces scratched and marred, bubbling in a container of acid to complete their destruction. In the cellar Dusty Fog waited to start the fire which would consume all the money already printed and the paper to make more. The printing-press had been ruined, inks, dyes and chemicals poured out of their containers.

"Ready, Belle?" he asked as the girl entered.

"When you are," she replied and passed a thick notebook to him. "Put this in your pocket. It's details of the entire business, what shipments they've sent off, where to, stuff like that."

"It'll be handy," Dusty admitted. "Willie and Jim've gone

up to clear those jaspers out of the house."

"I saw them," the girl smiled. "Willie's taking along a bottle of whisky he found, says it will cure his rheumatism—if he ever gets it."

"There's nothing like being prepared," Dusty grinned. "I'll start the fire, Belle. Get going."

By the door of the cellar Dusty rasped a match on his pants' seat and tossed it into the centre of the room. At first only a tiny finger of flame rose, but it grew by the second. A composition of benzole, coal tar, turpentine, residum and crude petroleum could be relied upon to burn well, as the makers of the incendiary shells from which it came knew. Watching the fire spread and grow, Dusty doubted if the Yankees would recover any part of their counterfeiting plant. To slow down any fire-fighting force which might arrive, Dusty spilled the last of the composition on the floor and up the cellar's wooden steps. Almost before he reached the top, he saw the first fingers of flame creeping after him.

All the lights were out in the hall by the time Dusty reached it. Already Bludso and Willie had dragged the bound and gagged Yankees from the house and far enough along the path to be safe should the whole house take fire. On Dusty joining them, the party hurried along to the main gates. So far no sign of the fire showed and muttered congratulations passed among the raiders.

Pulling open the gate, Jim Bludso allowed Belle to lead the way. Followed by Paupin, then Willie, the girl stepped on to St. Charles Avenue. Just too late she heard the grass-muffled feet of approaching men and saw several soldiers running towards her. By keeping to the wide, tree-dotted grass border of the street, the soldiers had escaped detection until almost too late.

Clearly the men came ready for trouble. Without challenging, the leader of the approaching party brought up his revolver and fired. Then a rifle cracked and its bullet struck the gate just in front of Dusty, causing him to take an involuntary pace to the rear. In doing so, he prevented Bludso from leaving.

"Run for it!" Belle shouted.

More shots rang out as the girl darted off along the street, closely followed by Willie and Paupin. Gun in hand, Dusty tried to go through the gate. Once again lead drove him back and a glance told him that there could be no leaving through the front entrance.

"We'll have to try the back, Jim!" he snapped, throwing a couple of shots at the rapidly approaching soldiers.

While Dusty did not hit any of them, he caused the soldiers to slow down. Turning, Dusty raced with Bludso along the path. Half of the soldiers approached the gates cautiously and the remainder charged by in hot pursuit of Belle's party. Already a small glow of fire showed in the house, but Dusty and Bludso ignored it. Hurdling the bound men, they ran along in front of the house, swung down the side and reached the rear. By sticking close to the wall again they avoided the chance of running into trip-wires and reached the rear gate. Although Dusty was prepared to shoot open the lock, the need did not arise.

"They'd got slack!" Bludso said. "The key's in the lock."

Swiftly the engineer turned the key and Dusty drew open the bolts. Opening the gate, they stepped out. Nobody challenged them, the narrow street at the rear of the house being deserted. Dusty transferred the key to the outside of the gate and turned it in the lock as Bludso closed the exit. With that done they moved off silently and could hear the first of their pursuers running towards the gate.

"It's locked!" yelled a voice. "They must still be in the grounds."

"Guard the gate, two of you," barked another. "The rest come with me to see if we can put out that fire."

"But those two—"

"Leave them. If they're roaming around the garden, we'll soon know it."

"Where now, Jim?" Dusty whispered.

"Back to the Busted Boiler as quick as we can. If I know Willie, he'll be taking Miss Belle and Saul there. Likely we'll meet up on the way."

Lead sang its eerie "splat!" sound around Belle's head as she ran along St. Charles Avenue, but none of it touched her. By keeping to the edge of the street, she and her companions offered a far harder target for the Yankee soldiers. The quarter moon did not give much light and the trees which lined the Avenue threw shadows not conducive to accurate shooting. Realising this, the soldiers stopped using their rifles and concentrated on running their quarry down.

The strenuous activities of the previous day and night, following upon a long journey in the cramped conditions aboard the *Jack* did not leave Belle in the best of physical condition. While Lucienne had shown her skill as a masseuse to remove most of the stiffness from Belle's bruised body that morning, she could not entirely eradicate the effects of the prize-fight. So the girl felt herself weakening. Discovering that they drew ahead of her, the two men slowed down.

"K—Keep going!" she gasped and tried to run faster.

Then her foot slipped on the projecting root of a tree and she stumbled. At another time she might have saved herself, but she moved too slowly. Bright lights seemed to be bursting in her head as she crashed into the tree's trunk and she slid down in a dazed, helpless heap to the ground.

Hearing Belle's cry of pain, Paupin and Willie skidded to a halt. Yells rose from the pursuing soldiers and one's rifle cracked. The bullet flung splinters from the tree, causing Paupin to stop as he went to help the girl. Bayonets glinted dully on the soldiers' rifles, a more deadly threat than bullets in the poor light. It would be certain capture, or death, to stay and fight; but to run away meant that Belle Boyd, the Rebel Spy, must fall into enemies' hands. Paupin realised that the result would be the same for Belle no matter which way he acted. However if he and Willie escaped to take the news to Dusty—always assuming the Yankees had not caught the small Texan—something might be done to rescue the girl. It was a slight chance, but better than no chance at all.

"Run, Willie!" he snapped, knowing what fate a Negro helping in such an affair could expect. "We've got to find Cap'n Fog."

Only for a moment did Willie hesitate. His thoughts on the matter ran parallel in all respects to Paupin's. So both men turned and ran on again, striding out at their best speed. Behind them, Belle tried to rise and to order them to save their own lives. Exhaustion welled through her and she became conscious of men around her and voices which seemed to come from a long way off reached her ears.

"One of 'em's down!" yelled the leading soldier, swinging his bayoneted Sharps rifle into an attack position.

Next moment another of the party jerked the cover from a bull's eye lantern he carried and illuminated Belle with its light.

"Hold that cat-stabber back," bawled a sergeant. "That's a woman."

Immediately the man with the ready bayonet held his thrust and the rest of the party came to a halt as they stared at Belle. Although the sergeant urged most of his men on after Paupin and Willie, the pause allowed the two men to increase their lead still more.

Slowly the dizziness left Belle and her eyes focused on the scene. Four soldiers formed a loose half circle in front of her, standing tense and watchful in the light of a lantern. Looking beyond them, Belle saw a trio of civilians approaching. The white bandage around the centre civilian's head identified him even before Belle could see his face. It seemed that Dusty's bullet had done less damage than they guessed, for Turnpike came towards Belle with his companions. At Turnpike's right side stalked a big, burly, bearded young man. The third of the group was smaller, thin, with a weak face and narrow, shifty eyes.

"So you managed to get one of them," growled the burly man, sweeping by the soldiers and bending over Belle. "Hey! It's a woman."

"I'd never've guessed," grunted the senior soldier present. "Reckon he must've learned things like that in college."

Although the burly civilian threw a savage glare at the soldier, he chose to ignore the comment. Instead he turned back to Belle and reached towards her hood. Suddenly he changed his hand's direction, shooting it down to grab her left wrist. Not until he had drawn the bracelet off did the bearded man offer to remove Belle's hood.

"We've got one of their big ones here, boys," the bearded man stated. "Only their best get these bracelets."

"What's wrong with the bracelet, Ike?" asked the smallest of the trio.

"I saw one of our men with his throat slit near on from ear to ear with one after he went to arrest Rose Greenhow," the bearded man answered. "This slut—."

"I recognise her!" Turnpike yelped, thrusting by the other. "She's the one who came to the shop."

"Are you sure, Melvin?" asked the bearded man.

"I'm sur—."

"Fire! Fire!"

At the sound of the two words shouted from along the street, Turnpike and his companions jerked around. A faint red glow showed over the wall around Gaton's property, growing brighter by the second.

"They've done it!" snarled the bearded man. "They've done it!"

"It wasn't my fault, Lorch!" Turnpike yelled back. "Damn it, you and Bartok know I did all I could."

When Turnpike had dashed from his office, he had failed to find any transport. Not fancying such a long walk, he had waited in the hope of seeing a passing hire hack, but none came. At last Lorch and Bartok, two more agents, returned in a carriage from making some investigation of their own. When Turnpike explained matters, the two men agreed to accompany him. On their arrival at the colonel's house, Turnpike met the guard commander and caused a further delay. Instead of telling the officer of his fears, Turnpike asked for the telegraph service to be tested. When no answer came, he knew that he guessed correctly. The guard turned out and moved fast, but too late as the fiery glow at Gaton's house showed.

"Get down there and see if you can save anything!" Lorch growled. "The safe ought to come through a fire and it's locked."

"I'll send some of the soldiers in to carry it out," Turnpike answered. "The officer of the guard has the key."

With that he turned and raced back towards the house. After watching Turnpike depart, Lorch took a pair of handcuffs from his jacket pocket and secured Belle's wrists behind her back. Then he hauled her roughly to her feet and gripped her right arm in his big left hand.

"You come quiet," he warned. "Make fuss for me and I'll break your arm. I'm not one of your Southern gentlemen and I don't think it's wrong to hit a woman."

"You'd probably find it easier and less dangerous than hitting a man," she replied and the soldiers chuckled.

"Easy there, college boy!" growled the oldest soldier as Lorch gave Belle a hard jerk. "I'm not Southern neither, but I don't stand for no man-handling a gal."

Nor did his companions if their low growls of agreement meant anything. So Lorch held down his anger at the interruption and started to walk towards the burning house. Belle went along, but she knew that she had never been in a tighter spot than at that moment.

Turning a corner which momentarily hid him from the following soldiers, Willie tore off his hood and threw it aside. "Keep going, Massa Saul!" he ordered. "Draw 'em off. I's a-going back to see if I can help Miss Belle or learn where they-all taking her."

"Where'll I go when I lose 'em?"

"Head back towards the Busted Boiler. If you go the way

we come, you ought to meet the others."

With that Willie swung behind a tree. Leaping up, he caught its lowest branch and hauled himself up. Hardly had the Negro swung his feet out of sight than the soldiers rushed around the corner. Paupin kept running at the fringe of the shadows and yelled as if encouraging his companion. Then the soldiers went by and Willie cautiously dropped to the ground. Taking the bottle of whisky from his pocket, he looked sadly at it.

"Lordy Lord!" he sighed, drawing the cork. "What a waste."

After splashing a liberal amount of the whisky on to his clothes, Willie filled his mouth and then spat it clear again. Moving carefully, he slipped across the street and stalked along in the shadows until close to the gates of the Gaton house. Assuming a drunken stagger, he walked across the street and when the two sentries at the gate saw him they concluded that he came from a house on the other side of the Avenue.

"W'a's going on, gents?" he inquired in a drunken voice, breathing whisky fumes into the nearest soldier's face.

"You'd best get going, Rastus," the soldier replied, drawing back a little. "It's none of your concern."

Willie saw Belle standing handcuffed inside the gate, but knew he could not hope to achieve anything in the way of a rescue. Playing for time, he pretended to be concerned about a cousin who worked at the house and watched Turnpike returning, followed by Bartok.

"They've bust open the safe!" Turnpike snarled. "Everything's gone. Killed Gaton, too."

"And he was the only one we've got who could make up the right inks," Bartok wailed. "It'll be months before we can get things going again. They may have found the record book, it wasn't in the safe."

"All right," Lorch answered, taking hold of Belle's head with one hand. "So we've got a mighty important prisoner here. She'll know where we can find the rest. Once we get back to our headquarters, we'll soon make her talk."

"It's not that easy," Turnpike warned. "That damned soldier told his officer about the girl. The stupid, sentimental old fool insists she's his prisoner and insists we hand her over to him."

"Like hell!" Lorch barked.

"You aiming to argue it with him?" Turnpike inquired. "He says we're not to torture her and that if we try it, he'll stop us."

"He might, if he found us at it," Lorch answered. "We'll take her—."

"He knows where our headquarters is," Bartok interrupted.

"And that's where he'll go looking for her," Lorch replied. "Only she won't be there. We'll take her to—."

"Madam Lucienne's shop," Turnpike put in. "There'll be nobody around and I've got a key. While we're at it, we may as well learn if there's anything in the shop. She may know."

"The shop it is then," barked Lorch.

While talking, the men had been walking Belle along. Suddenly they became aware that somebody followed them. Turning, the men looked at Willie who wobbled uncertainly along in their wake. A white man would have been immediately suspect, but none of the trio connected a Negro with Belle.

"Where're you going?" Lorch demanded.

"I'se been to a marrying and's going home, sah," Willie answered, breathing a cloud of whisky fumes into the bearded face. "Down that ways, sah."

As Willie had taken an opportunity to wash his mouth out again, Lorch did not doubt his drunken appearance. Watching Willie stagger off, Lorch gave a snort.

"Do you reckon he's all right?" Bartok asked.

"He's drunk," Lorch answered. "Come on, let's get the carriage. The soldier reckons they've two of the rebs cornered in the garden and he's setting up sentries to keep them in until morning. We've time to be on our way before he misses us."

"He'll never think of looking for us at the shop," Turnpike purred, laying a hand on Belle's shoulder and sinking his fingers into her flesh. "I'm looking forward to this."

Belle did not reply. Not a flicker of expression had she allowed her recognition of Willie to show. Darting a glance over her shoulder while pretending to free herself from Turnpike's grasp, Belle saw that the Negro had already disappeared into the alley between two houses. While she guessed that Willie was going as fast as he could to fetch help, Belle wondered where he might find it.

Cursing the officer of the guard for his insistence that they did not torture the girl, Turnpike, Lorch and Bartok hustled her back to the big house from which they came. On arrival they found that a well-meaning servant had un-hitched, fed and watered the two horses from the carriage. Calling the man a number of things—but not a poor, down-trodden victim of the vicious rebels, their usual term for a Negro—Bartok and Turnpike went to re-harness the team. Although only Lorch remained with her, Belle knew better than try to escape. The bearded man watched her too carefully and was so powerful that she could not hope to defeat him with her hands secured behind her back.

With the horses hitched, Bartok took the driver's seat and his companions placed themselves on either side of Belle in the back. The quickest way to Madam Lucienne's shop would have taken them by the front of the Gaton house, but Lorch ordered Bartok to turn in the other direction. If the officer saw them leave that way, he would think they were going to their headquarters. Long before he learned his mistake, Lorch expected to have gained all the information possible from the girl. After that it would be up to Allen Pinkerton, as head of the Secret Service, to make excuses to the Army.

"What's your name?" Lorch growled as the carriage clattered through the darkened streets.

"Martha Lincoln," Belle replied. "You may know my husband, Abraham."

"Have your fun while you can, girlie," Turnpike snarled.

"She's a spunky little devil, that's for sure," Lorch went on and laid his hand on Belle's thigh. When she tried to pull away, he grinned at her. "Don't worry, peach-blossom, there's not enough room here."

With that, he nipped the tender flesh on the inside of her thigh. Only with an effort did Belle hold down a gasp of pain. She felt afraid, more so than ever in her life, as the man released his hold. All too well she knew what kind of men held her in their power. Young intellectuals, well-educated, but with all the bigotry and intolerance of their kind, hating all Southerners for daring to oppose their beliefs, the trio would not hesitate to torture her, or worse, if they could do so without risk to themselves.

Belle wondered what had happened to Dusty and Bludso. Although the Yankees believed the two rebels to be in the garden, Belle doubted it. Knowing the dangers, Dusty and Bludso would not stay in the house's grounds unless they had no way out. She did not dare try to raise her hopes by imagining the two men would be able to effect a rescue.

No chance of escape presented itself during the drive to Lucienne's shop, despite the fact that it took twice as long as it should. Given a practical piece of work, Bartok proved sadly lacking in ability. When it became apparent that Bartok was lost, Lorch insisted they stop and ask a passing patrol for directions. Even then the bearded man found it necessary to keep a check on Bartok to prevent him from taking a wrong turn.

At last the carriage rolled along the dark, deserted Le Havre Street and halted outside Lucienne's shop. Climbing down, Turnpike took a key from his pocket and went to the shop's door. While Lorch and Bartok made Belle leave the carriage, Turnpike entered the shop. He found and lit a lamp, standing it on the counter.

Bringing Belle in, Lorch shoved her on to a straight-

backed chair. He bent her torso forward until he could haul
her arms over the back of the chair and growled orders to
his companions. Held in such a manner Belle could not
struggle and Bartok brought a length of stout cord which
Lorch used to fasten the handcuff's links to the rear legs of
the chair.

"You're going to talk now, peach-blossom," he told her
and gripped the neck of her shirt.

With a savage jerk Lorch ripped the shirt down the front.
He continued pulling and tearing until Belle sat naked to
the waist. Lust showed on all the trio's faces as they stared
at the round swell of her bust.

"You've been in the wars, peach-blossom," Lorch purred,
fingering the mottling of bruises on her ribs. "I thought you
messed up your face when you fell against the tree. Who
did it?"

"Maybe it was some nigger she used to mistreat as a
slave," Turnpike sneered, eyes fixed as if by a magnet to
her naked torso.

"Whoever it was, she proved a damned sight tougher
than you," Belle hissed.

"Why you—!" Turnpike began, lunging forward with
the intention of driving his fist into her face.

Belle kicked up, hoping to catch him where it would do
the most good. Instead of striking his groin, her boot collided with his shin. Letting out a howl, he hopped on the
other leg and clutched at his pain-filled limb. Then he flung
himself back just in time to avoid a second kick. Almost
foaming at the mouth in his rage, Turnpike drew his Smith
& Wesson and lined it at the girl.

"Quit that!" Lorch bellowed, shoving Turnpike's gun-
arm aside. "If you kill her, we'll learn nothing."

"Let me work on her face with the butt then!" Turnpike
snarled.

"Not just yet," Lorch answered and moved around to
where Belle could not kick him. Cupping his hand almost

gently under her left breast, he flicked its nipple with his thumb. "Let's try another way first."

"Get your filthy Yankee hands off me!" Belle said and the contempt in her voice raked Lorch like a whip. "I'd as soon be mauled by a pig."

Drawing back a pace before the raw scorn showed by the girl, Lorch glared at her for a moment. Then he slashed his left hand around, driving the back of it viciously into Belle's bust. The girl's body stiffened and she could not stop a cry of agony bursting from her lips.

CHAPTER FIFTEEN

A Man Who Deserved to Die

"There's somebody coming, Jim," Dusty Fog said as they stood in a dark alley some distance from the Gaton house. "Only one man, travelling fast."

"It's not a soldier either," Bludso guessed. "Maybe it's one of the others."

After slipping out of Gaton's back garden, Dusty and Bludso had not been followed by the Yankees. They heard the shooting on St. Charles Avenue and wondered how their friends fared. Knowing they could do nothing to help at that moment, Dusty and Bludso reluctantly made their way towards the first of the prearranged rendezvous points. There they waited in the hope that all of their friends might join them. Silence had fallen in the direction of Gaton's house, at least as far as shooting went. A red glow grew higher in the sky and the two men heard distant yelling as soldiers fought the fire.

While waiting Dusty reloaded his Colt's two empty chambers, working deftly with only an occasional need for

Bludso to light a match and illuminate his work. By the time they heard the approaching footsteps, Dusty once more held a gun with six full and capped chambers.

Coming up to the waiting pair, Paupin wondered how they would take the news that he escaped while Belle fell into the Yankees' hands and Willie returned to try a rescue. Quickly he told Dusty and Bludso the full story, expecting to hear savage condemnation when he finished.

"You did the right thing, Saul," Dusty said quietly. "If they'd taken you all, it would have been a long time before we heard about it."

"And Willie stands a better chance than any of us to get close to Belle," Bludso went on. "What do you reckon, Dusty?"

"That we make a stab at saving Belle. What'll Willie do?"

"Learn what he can, do whatever he can. If he sees he can't save her, he'll try to find out where they're taking her."

"We'll need help, likely," Dusty said. "Let's give him ten minutes to come here, then head back to the Busted Boiler and make plans."

"It'd be best," agreed Bludso. "Anybody after you, Saul?"

"Nope. I led them around to draw them away from Willie, then lost them and cut back this way."

"We'll give him ten minutes then," Dusty decided.

Never had time dragged so slowly as during the minutes Dusty stood in the dark alley. The mission had been a success, with the counterfeiting plant destroyed, its operator dead and details of the whole scheme in the small Texan's pocket. It would be a long time before the Yankees could make a reorganisation of the size needed to start the counterfeiting chain from printer to distributors and before then the Confederate Government could take precautions. Many people would regard the affair a success should Dusty make good his escape with the news; but he could not go and leave Belle a prisoner. He must at least make some determined attempt to rescue the girl, even at the risk of his own life and freedom.

"We'd best go, Dusty," Bludso said gently.

"I suppose so," Dusty answered in a disappointed voice, knowing the time to be up. "Willie'll foll—."

At that moment they heard the padding of feet approaching and fell silent. Breathing hard, Willie loped up to the trio and halted to lean on the wall. After a few seconds, the Negro looked first at Saul Paupin then to the other two men.

"See you made it, Massa Saul."

"What'd you learn, Willie?" Dusty put in.

"Miss Belle's in bad trouble, Cap'n. Three fellers done took her off in a carriage."

"Soldiers?"

"Naw. They was some of Pinkerton's men. Leastwise one of 'em was. I'd know his whiskery face any ole time, Cap'n. He's a mean one, real bad. 'Nother of 'em looked like somebody done whomped his ole pumpkin head with a club, way it was all bandaged up."

"That'll be Turnpike, Dusty," Bludso growled. "I thought you'd shot him up real bad."

"There wasn't time to take careful aim," Dusty explained. "Happen I get another crack at him I won't make the same mistake."

"I'd say they'll be taking Belle to their headquarters for questioning," Paupin put in.

"They ain't," Willie answered. "Seems like the Yankee officer of the guard figured they aimed to abuse Miss Belle real bad and wouldn't have it. So they done snuck off someplace to work on her secret-like."

"Do you know where, Willie?"

Although the words left Dusty in a soft, almost gentle whisper, they brought a chill to all the listeners.

"They allowed to take her to Madam Lucienne's shop," Willie answered.

"Let's get going!" Bludso growled.

"Not you, Jim," Dusty replied. "One way or another

there'll be a big hunt for us by tomorrow dawn at the earliest. If I rescue Belle, the sooner she's out of New Orleans the better. If not—well, it'd be best if the *Jack*'s gone by morning."

"So?" Bludso asked.

"I want you to go to the Busted Boiler, get Belle's and my gear and take them to the *Jack*. Tell Cord Pinckney to be ready and pull out by three in the morning whether we're there or not."

"How about you?"

"Willie can get me to the shop, Jim. I reckon we can handle three like Turnpike. There's no time to argue it, anyway."

Bludso knew Dusty spoke the truth. Already a messenger would be rushing to the Garrison Commander and most likely New Orleans would be swarming with Federal soldiers searching for the party who had destroyed a valuable piece of Union property. So far no organised effort had been made by the Yankees, but each minute drew them closer to when it would be.

"How about me, Captain?" Paupin inquired.

"Stay with Jim. He'll hide you until we can have you moved out of town and to somewhere safe."

"I'll get you on to a foreign boat when one comes in with a skipper I can trust," Bludso promised.

"Damn it, I'm not bothered about that!" the safe-breaker barked. "I meant what can I do to help Miss Boyd?"

"Go with Jim, Saul," Dusty said gently. "If I can't get to Belle, he'll maybe need an expert at opening locks."

"That's for sure," Bludso admitted. "Let's go, Saul."

"I'll maybe not run across you again, Saul," Dusty said, offering his hand to the man. "But if there's ever anything I can do for you, just get word to me."

With his hand tingling from Dusty's grip, Paupin watched the small Texan fade off into the darkness at Willie's side.

"There goes the biggest man I know," the safe-breaker remarked.

"He's all of that," Bludso agreed. "Let's go. I've an idea of my own and you can help me on it."

Guided by Willie, Dusty passed through the streets of old New Orleans but at the rear of its stately mansions. By following the routes used by coloured servants, they avoided the notice of soldiers heading towards the Gaton place. When reaching Le Harve Street, on which stood Madam Lucienne's shop, Dusty and Willie found it deserted. However a carriage stood before her establishment and a light showed through its front windows.

"They're here, 'cap'n," Willie breathed. "That's their carriage."

"Let's go then," Dusty replied, Colt sliding into his hand.

Silently they moved along the sidewalk and Dusty peeped around the edge of the window. Behind him, Willie heard a low growl of rage. Then Dusty went by the window and the Negro looked in to see Lorch drive a hand at Belle's naked bust. Even as the blow landed, Dusty hurled himself like a living projectile at the shop's door.

With Belle's scream ringing in his ears, Dusty burst into the room and his coming took the three Yankees by surprise. So completely had their attention been on Belle that none of them heard or saw Dusty pass the window. They did not even suspect his presence until the door flew open and then it was too late.

For once in his young life Dusty allowed anger to override thought in a dangerous situation. By his treatment of the helpless Belle, Lorch was a man who deserved to die; but he did not hold a gun and so presented less of a danger than the armed Turnpike. Normally Dusty would have dealt with Turnpike first, but the expression of pain on Belle's face caused him to forget that elementary precaution.

Even as shock and fear wiped the lust-filled sneer from Lorch's bearded features, Dusty shot him in the head. Although the bullet would have done a satisfactory job, Dusty thumbed off a second on its heels. Lorch pitched backwards, struck the counter and slid to the floor as dead as a man could be with a .44 bullet ranging upwards through each eye.

Terror knifed into Turnpike as he recognised the small Texan. Seeing the manner in which Lorch died did nothing to lessen Turnpike's fears. Having twice witnessed the Texan's superlative skill in handling a gun, Turnpike had no wish to try conclusions with Dusty again. A way out of the difficulty presented itself close to hand and Turnpike took it, fast. Lunging forward, he thrust the muzzle of his Smith & Wesson against the side of Belle's head.

"I'll kill the girl!" he yelled in a voice high with fear.

Dusty took in the situation rapidly. At Belle's right side stood a man so scared that he might pull his gun's trigger in blind panic. To her left, Bartok—no less scared-looking—reached for the Colt Baby Dragoon in his jacket pocket. With Belle's life and his own as the stake, Dusty knew he must handle the matter just right. Swiftly he studied the two men, assessing their natures and forming his conclusions. Even as Belle opened her mouth to advise him to go ahead and shoot, Dusty acted—although not in the manner she would have expected.

Giving a dejected, beaten shrug, the small Texan reached up with his left hand to take hold of the Colt by its cylinder. Still wearing the attitude of a man thoroughly whipped, he reversed the Colt with his left forefinger through the triggerguard. Supporting the gun lightly on his remaining fingers, he offered it butt pointing upwards towards Turnpike.

"I surrender. My name is Captain Dusty Fog, Texas Light Cavalry, and I demand the privileges of my rank as a prisoner-of-war."

A mixture of rage and hate twisted at Turnpike's face as he listened to the words. Before him stood one of the people responsible for wrecking a scheme designed to bring the South's economy crashing into such ruins that it would be unlikely ever to recover, even if such misguided fools as President Lincoln offered the chance, as seemed likely, after the War. The utter and complete destruction of the hated

white Southerners had been the aim behind the plan when
formulated by Turnpike and others of his kind, not merely
the bringing about of a speedy and less bloody ending to
the War.

Nor did Dusty's part in destroying the counterfeiting plant
form Turnpike's only reason for hatred. The small Texan
had proven himself more capable than the Yankee agent and
had performed deeds that the other knew he could not hope
even to approach. Like all his kind, Turnpike hated any
man who did something he could not and Dusty's small,
insignificant appearance made matters worse.

The sight of the Texan standing in an attitude of abject
surrender drove some of Turnpike's fear away. Then a thought
struck the Yankee. Already that night he had seen one ex-
ample of military chivalry, in the officer of the guard's
determination that no ill-treatment should come the female
prisoner's way. A man with Captain Dusty Fog's reputation
could expect good treatment from most Federal regular soldiers, who would have respect for a brave and honourable
enemy. Nothing so lenient must be allowed to happen. Alive,
Dusty Fog could testify to their treatment of the girl. Far
worse, he would be living proof of Turnpike's inadequacy
and failure.

With that thought in mind, Turnpike swung the Smith &
Wesson's barrel away from Belle's head and played right
into Dusty's hands. Gambling on Turnpike's knowledge of
firearms being, by Texas standards, rudimentary, Dusty prepared to try a move often practiced but never used in earnest
by him until that moment.

When reversing the gun in apparent surrender, Dusty left
its hammer drawn back at full cock. The lack of objection
to the state of his gun by Turnpike or Bartok increased the
small Texan's confidence. With the Smith & Wesson turning
away from Belle, all Dusty needed to do was get the Colt's
butt into his hand and squeeze its trigger.

Professional duellists had discovered how twirling and
spinning a pistol on its triggerguard strengthened the fingers

and helped develop increased accuracy. The information passed West, where men frequently found the need for skilled use of a hand gun under less formal conditions than the *code duello*. During spells of gun-juggling, Dusty developed a trick later to become famous, or notorious, as "the road-agent's spin." It was a trick of desperation, and one only likely to work, even before its latter-day publicity, against a man lacking in knowledge of practical gun-handling matters.

Waiting until the Smith & Wesson passed out of line with Belle's head, Dusty gave his left hand a slight jerk upwards. At the same moment he released his hold of the barrel with his other fingers. With his forefinger as its pivot, the Colt's butt rose upwards and curled over to slap into his waiting palm. Instantly Dusty's remaining three fingers folded around the curved bone grip and he squeezed the trigger with unhurried speed.

Too late Turnpike saw his danger. Being unable to use his gun left-handed, it never occurred to him that others might be able to do so. Nor did he possess the kind of lightning fast reactions which might have saved him. Flame ripped from the barrel of Dusty's Colt and a bullet tore into Turnpike's chest. Reeling under the impact, the Yankee retained his hold of the Smith & Wesson. Again Dusty fired, angling his shot upwards. The bullet ripped into Turnpike's throat, sending him backwards and the gun clattered from his hand as he fell.

Terror lent speed to Bartok's movements and he had spent more time than his companions at learning to handle a revolver. Jerking out his small Colt, he swung it up to line at Dusty. Belle saw there would be no time for Dusty to deal with both Turnpike and Bartok, so took a hand in the game. Using all her strength, she flung herself and the chair over to crash into Bartok's side. A yelp of surprise left the man and his Colt jerked aside just as it fired. Hearing the shot, Dusty swung from firing his second shot at Turnpike.

One glance warned the small Texan that he faced a man with some gun-skill. Enough for there to be no taking chances with him.

Cocking the little Colt smoothly, Bartok prepared to shoot again. Dusty threw himself to one side, dropping to the ground. As he landed, the small Texan lined up his Colt and missed death by inches as the Baby Dragoon spat out another .31 ball. Once again Dusty found himself in a position where he must shoot to make an instant kill. So he took that extra split-second necessary to aim. Then the Colt bucked in his palm, its deep roar echoing in challenge to the lighter crack of the small calibre weapon in Bartok's hand. Driving up, the bullet Dusty fired tore into the soft flesh beneath Bartok's jaw, passing on upwards through the roof of his mouth and into the brain. Dusty did what he had to do, achieved an instant kill, and Bartok's body collapsed like an unstuffed rag doll across Belle's legs.

Partially winded by landing on the floor, her fastened arms prevented any chance of breaking the fall, Belle lay gasping in pain. Willie burst into the room as Dusty rose and together they approached the girl. Bending down, the two men lifted the girl and the chair upright.

"Are you all right, Belle?" Dusty asked.

"I've felt better," she admitted. "The bearded one has the key."

While Willie used a cut-throat razor to sever the cord holding Belle to the chair, Dusty searched Lorch's body and recovered the key to the handcuffs. On her wrists being freed, Belle gasped and raised her right hand to rub at the left shoulder. Then she remembered the state of her clothing and tried to cover up her naked torso. Dusty thrust the Colt into his waistband and removed his jacket to give to the girl. Slipping into it, Belle glanced at Willie as the Negro went to the shop's door and stood listening.

"We'd best get going, Cap'n," he said. "There's folks coming a-running and they's wearing heavy boots."

"Can you walk, Belle?" Dusty asked.

"I'm game to try," she replied. "Let's get going. Out of the back way, too."

Although the building had been thoroughly searched, Turnpike's men did not trouble to take away the back door's key. Belle followed Dusty's action in locking the door after them on leaving. Already they could hear running feet drawing closer to the shop, but not from its rear. Darting a quick glance around, Belle suggested that Willie take them by the least conspicuous route to the Busted Boiler.

"There's no need for that," Dusty told her. "Jim's collected our gear and he'll be taking it to the *Jack*. We've done what we came for, Belle. It's time we got out of New Orleans."

CHAPTER SIXTEEN

A Way of Life

Dawn crept greyly into the eastern sky and Lieutenant Cord Pinckney watched the ever-growing light with care. Although they had crept by the main New Orleans' up-river defences, there was always the chance of meeting some U.S. Navy craft returning from a journey. Or if a chance-passing cavalry patrol happened to see them from the shore, it would only be a matter of hours at most before a fast launch or two came after them.

On arrival at the hidden dock, Dusty, Belle and Willie found everything ready. Each night, when the smoke would not be seen rising from among the ruins, Pinckney's men built enough fire to raise a head of steam capable of giving the *Jack* motive power. So they needed only to pole their vessel out from under its hiding place and set off up-river.

Already the alarm had been raised and the first part of a massive search campaign begun. While the main body of men concentrated on the area around Gaton's house, the U.S. Navy started to put out guard boats on the river so

thickly that sneaking through them in the *Jack,* even ballasted down to the limits of safety, invited disaster.

Jim Bludso came up with the answer. In fact he had been
preparing for it through his return to the Busted Boiler and
carrying the gear to the dock. Once he had delivered the
two bags and given Dusty's message to Pinckney, Bludso
told the lieutenant of his own idea. Before the others arrived,
Bludso left to put the plan into operation. With the aid of
Paupin and three trusted men from the Busted Boiler, Bludso
stole a steam launch used as picket boat by the Yankee fleet,
making sure that the theft would be discovered quickly. Then
he and his men headed downstream as if trying to escape
through to the sea. Rockets flamed into the air and steam
whistles whooped a warning, drawing guard boats and such
larger craft as had enough steam up to follow down river
and away from the *Jack.*

Timing their moves just right, Bludso's men abandoned
the stolen launch and left it tearing along with a locked tiller
to be sunk by shell fire from the pursuing vessels. After
swimming ashore, Bludso and his party made good their
escape. While the Yankees searched for survivors, and eventually concluded that the launch went down with all hands,
the *Jack* passed up-river unnoticed.

The journey north took longer than coming down to New
Orleans. There could be no travelling by day under a pile
of bushes as that would only attract attention. So at dawn
each day the *Jack* halted at the first suitable spot and hid
in some way until darkness left them free to move on again.
Clearly the Yankees did not suspect their method of escape,
for no search of the up-river side of New Orleans was made.

At last they turned off the Mississippi and up the Red
River. Despite being in comparatively safe waters, Pinckney
waited until nightfall before trying to reach Alexandria. So
far the Yankees did not know of the *Jack's* presence on the
Upper Mississippi and he wanted to keep it that way. So he
chanced dangers of passing through the spar-torpedo field
in the darkness rather than make an appearance in the city's

dock area during daylight and in view of possible Yankee spies.

Dusty and Belle landed at the same lagoon from which they embarked. Nor did they waste time in celebrating their successful mission. As soon as she could arrange, Belle and Dusty boarded a sidewheel riverboat and carried on with their trip to rejoin Ole Devil.

"You've done well, Miss Boyd, Dustine," said the General in a grim satisfaction as he listened to their report. "And how about your friends?"

"I don't know, sir," Belle admitted. "You've heard nothing?"

"Not a thing."

After the War Dusty learned that Madam Lucienne and Paupin made good their departure on a British ship after being kept hidden by Bludso until the Yankees gave up an extensive search for the wreckers of the counterfeiting plant. No suspicion fell on Bludso, although Pinkerton himself conducted an investigation into the deaths of Turnpike's party. For the rest of the War Bludso served the South well and with peace returned to being a riverboat engineer on a new Prairie Belle.

Not that Dusty and Belle knew anything of their friends as they sat in Ole Devil's office on their return.

"Any news for me, General?" asked the girl.

"You're to go as soon as possible to Atlanta," Ole Devil replied. "Dustine, that damned guerilla Hannah's come into our area again. Tomorrow you'll take your company, a sharpshooter and mountain howitzer and bring in the whole stinking bunch."

A mission had been completed at great risk, but that did not end the War. Short of men, Ole Devil could not afford the luxury of keeping his favourite nephew and a full company of men sitting idle.

"I'll be gone when you come back, Dustine," the girl said as she and the small Texan left the office. "Thanks for everything."

"What'll you be doing in Atlanta, Belle?" he inquired.

"I'll not know until I reach there."

"Why don't you give it up while you can, Belle?" Dusty said. "You nearly lost your life this time."

"I can't give it up. It's in my blood, Dusty. Lord knows what I'll do when the War's over. There'll be no more need for me or my talents then."

And Belle laughed. Neither she nor Dusty realised that the War would soon be over; or how there would still in peace be work for the Rebel Spy.

Author's note: *For details of Dusty's hunt after Hannah's Guerillas and his next meeting with the Rebel Spy, read THE BAD BUNCH.*